The Man in the Mud Room

A Callum Lange Mystery

Nicola Pearson

This story is a work of fiction.
No part of the contents relate to any real person or persons, living or dead.

ISBN-13: 978-1511577793
ISBN-10: 1511577797

Acknowledgements

Once again I'm grateful to Detective Theresa Luvera of the Skagit County Sheriff's Office for helping me with the facts about detective work. Thanks also to Vicki Johnson for talking to me about wildcrafting, Jerry Ziegler and Donald Drummond for starting and finishing the edits to this manuscript, Mary Ann Wisman and Mary Machala for proofing it and Carole Schaefer for giving me things to think about. Thanks also to my husband, Stephen Murray, for relating interesting tidbits that he hears when he's out about about in our community. They put color in my stories.

Cover Art:

Original photograph of The October Hunters' Moon over Sauk Mountain taken by Adrienne Smith. Graphic design by Jon-Paul Verfaillie.

For my mother,
with love.

Callum Lange's stride didn't vary as he climbed the last few feet towards his property. It used to take him 40 minutes to make the walk from the highway up to the gate but now he could do it easily in 20. Well usually in 20 but today he was carrying a pack with his groceries in it as well as his laptop, his mail, and a couple of tomes by Jared Diamond he'd picked up at the library so maybe he'd been slower. He pulled his cell phone out of the waist pocket of his purple fleece jacket to double check his time and saw that he'd missed a call. He stopped, wondering who had thought to call him, then edged forward slowly as he peered down at the number. It was a 360 area code, so local, but he didn't recognize the number. He grunted surprise low in his chest.

At the gate to his property he stopped again, feeling the chill of the October air on the tip of his nose, and debated calling the number back while he still had cell phone reception. He thought about the pint of s'mores flavored ice cream in his backpack and the letter from his ex-partner on the job in NYC, which he was curious to read. He also thought about the game of Pirateer in his yurt that he was playing with Suleka and the fact that he was only 45 minutes shy of their self-imposed time limit to make a move. He peered at his cell phone again, wondering if it was Suleka who had called him, but her number ended in 24 not 77. Lange didn't have any of his contacts stored in his smart phone because he figured it would help keep his brain cells limber to have them all memorized.

He slipped the phone back into his pocket, having decided the call could wait, and scissored his legs over the 15-foot long gate to his property. Walking down the gently curving, gently undulating, quarter mile long dirt road that led into the flattest section of his 80 acres, Lange listened to the songbirds around him as he thought about the last time he and his partner, Jimmy Vonortas, had seen each other.

It was Lange's final day of work for NYPD and he was cleaning out his desk when Jimmy, who'd been temporarily suspended for shooting a suspect that was fleeing the scene, burst into the squad room. "You're leaving?" asked his Greek-American partner, both hands out at his sides in a how-could-this-be gesture.

"I told you I was retiring," Lange answered.

"Yes, but you're *leaving*?!" Vonortas insisted, coming around the desk despite himself to help throw Lange's personal items into a box.

Lange shrugged. "I'm flying out to Washington tomorrow, yes."

"How can you? How can you leave New York?"

They'd had this discussion many times and Callum Lange was tired of hearing about how he could buy ice cream at two in the morning in Manhattan, a concept that didn't interest him in the least. But Jimmy Vonortas was about 20 years Lange's junior and even though they'd been partners just over a year, what they'd gone through together with the shooting had bonded the young man to him. "If you only knew where I was going," Lange sighed.

Jimmy threw his taut, athletic body down into a hardback chair next to the desk and slid forward so his torso was at an angle to the seat. "Yeah, I know, I know, the Magic Skagit!" he growled. "You don't even know why it's called that."

The older detective sucked on his dentures a moment before replying. "Nobody does," he said softly. "That's what makes it magic."

That had been a year and four months ago. Since then he and Vonortas had e-mailed a few times, mostly about the investigation, but it was always stilted, impersonal. A handwritten letter though – well, that had the potential to be different. Lange looked down, suddenly aware that his right hand had drifted up to the spot by his left shoulder; even through the fleece he could feel the hard, wrinkled skin of the scar.

A strong, high-pitched, fluty call to his right took his mind out of New York City and into the forest around him. He stopped, mid-stride, and ran his eyes over the trees alongside the road. There he was, sitting on the branch of a Doug fir; a bright yellow-breasted, red-headed Western Tanager. Lange felt a surge of regret that he didn't have a pair of binoculars with him to get a closer look at this beautiful little bird. What he needed was a small, high quality pair that would live in his pocket for just this kind of occasion. The regret quickly dissipated with his enjoyment of the bird's throaty, repetitive chirp ch-chirp ch-chirp ch-chirp.

Lange stood for a few verses then took off down the road again, buoyed by his constant amazement that he was lucky enough to live in such a place. In fact, he was so pumped he almost missed the footprints in the wet mud.

But he didn't. As soon as his eyes caught them, he stopped and bent forward, glad that this one section of his road almost never dried out, shaded as it was by tall trees on both sides. Curiously the footprints only went in one direction, towards him. This suggested that whoever made them had left by this road but not come in this way. Unless they'd just skirted the wet ground on the way in. Didn't make a lot of sense for them not to skirt it again on the way out, Lange thought to himself. But then he'd met a lot of people whose actions didn't make sense.

He crouched down and stared at the telltale tracks in the dark, shiny, muddy circle splayed across the center of his road. He tipped his head to the right, then the left, and narrowed his eyes. There were three different footprints in the mud, each one well-defined. He was pretty sure he could determine the brand and size of the shoes that made them. Maybe even the idiosyncratic walking patterns of the person wearing them. He huffed to himself; in NYC he could do that, or even better, have someone do it for him. Out here, he'd have to look up shoe soles on the Internet and keep searching until he found a match. Since he'd just been to the local library to do what he wanted online, he wasn't about to go back.

He spread the fingers of his right hand apart and used the distance between his thumb and his pinkie to guesstimate the length of each print. Two were longer than his spread hand - considerably longer - and when he held his hand against the length of his own foot he found the same to be true. The third footprint was smaller. So maybe two guys and a woman, Lange thought to himself, or two adult males and a kid? None of the footprints had a deep tread pattern so Lange guessed they were made by sneakers, not hiking boots. He stood up and reflected a moment. Most likely it was teenagers, using his place to drink. Or smoke. Or both.

He edged around the wet ground, heading for his yurt, then changed his mind. He pulled his smart phone out of his pocket and snapped a quick photo of the prints. Just in case. Then he walked on. He was still conscious of the timeline on his move in Pirateer, plus he wanted to see if there was further evidence of this visit his property had been paid. The one thing he really hoped was that if they'd come to party, they'd taken home the empties. The thought of litter set his teeth on edge.

At the end of the road, the land opened up to a wide, rugged plateau with views out over the valley below. Lange's yurt was directly ahead, with the door facing him and one half of its circle nestled up against the trees. The other half, which held the only window in the entire canvas wall, faced out towards the rest of the ledge and the view. Nothing looked disturbed, as far as he could tell from the outside. He veered to the right and eyeballed a simple pole building he'd erected late in the summer to house his John Deere tractor and lawn mower, as well as sundry other items he was accumulating for his future log cabin. His searched the ground in front of the building, for signs of possible trespass, but it looked undisturbed; and his tractor, chainsaw and tools inside the structure, under the blue metal roof, were untouched.

Lange strode forward, his lithe, six foot one frame moving comfortably, easily, across the uneven terrain as his Red Wings scrunched through the woody ground cover. He slowed when he reached his log pile and walked a lazy rectangle around the perimeter, looking for empty beer cans. But there was none. Satisfied, but still curious, he began the journey over to his yurt.

Dusk was descending on his mountain hollow and as Lange tried to rub the cold away from the end of his nose, he pictured a cheery fire in his woodstove. He walked past the steps leading up to his door and over to his long, tidy stacks of firewood. He contemplated just grabbing an armload but when he thought about how toasty he could get inside with the fire going, he decided to get enough for the entire evening. He walked around the wheelbarrow, which was lying upside down on the ground at the end of the stacks, and bent forward to grab the handles so he could flip it right side up. That's when he noticed the hole in the rows of firewood at the back of his stacks. Dammit, he thought, somebody *is* getting at my wood! Just last week he'd dumped a bucket load of cut and split alder out of his tractor onto the ground over here, thinking he'd add it to the stacks, but when he came back to it a couple of days later, the pile looked smaller. Except dumped like that and covered with a tarp, he couldn't be sure. Now a U-shaped hole under the sheet metal on his furthest, driest stack made him sure.

What he didn't understand was, why *his* firewood, so far up the mountain? And why on foot?

*****

Lange filled the wheelbarrow with pinkish-yellow wedges of Doug fir. He would enjoy the snapping sounds it made as it burned and he hoped it would take his mind off the fact that someone had been on his property, pilfering his firewood. He lifted the handles and was halfway over to his yurt when he was interrupted by the cell phone jangling in his pocket. It so startled him, lost in thought as he was and not knowing that he had cell phone reception here on his property, that he dropped the wheelbarrow and narrowly missed having it land on his foot. "What?!" he barked into the phone.

"Am I bothering you?!" a female voice barked back at him.

"Nobut...."

"So that's how you always answer the phone?"

"Whatareyou.....," Lange stuttered, then regained his composure. "Who *is* this?!"

"It's Suleka!"

"It doesn't sound like Suleka."

"It doesn't? How should I sound then?"

"Okay, maybe it does now," conceded Lange. "You were distorted before."

"I'm always distorted but that's beside the point."

"Very funny," grumbled Lange. Then he remembered something. "Did you call earlier?"

"No." Suleka paused but went on when Lange didn't fill the void. "Did you get Detective Deller's message?"

"Frankie left me a message?"

"Yes."

"Well then no. But you know I don't usually get cell phone reception up here. The fact that you're getting through now is kind of an anomaly."

"Is that why you bit my head off when you answered? You were so blown away that you got cell service?"

"No, I was blown away that I didn't break my foot by dropping a load of firewood on it when my phone rang!"

"Are you hurt?"

"Well, no...."

"You want me to call back so you can try again? Give you a reason to whine?"

"Now you are bothering me," Lange complained and just as quickly, changed the subject. "Say, do you know anything about someone stealing my firewood?"

"Nooooo!" Suleka dragged the word out, filling it with concern, and Lange could picture her brown eyes softening and her thick, dark brows coming together the way they did when she heard something that disturbed her. "Somebody stole your firewood? How did they get past your gate?"

"They walked, which limited how much they could steal...." He heard a small gasp from her end. "What?"

"People have been talking about a rash of small thefts on Hwy 530, which isn't that far from you."

"Small thefts? Like what exactly?"

"A can opener, a quart of milk, beans that were soaking in a pot on the stove..."

Lange tipped his head up, thinking about this. It was almost dark now and the motion sensor light over his door popped on as a bug flew past it.

"Cal? Are you still there?"

"Yes, yes, I'm here," Lange replied. His mind wanted to chew over the information she'd just given him but he knew it couldn't until he stopped being on the phone with her. "Why did you call me?" he asked suddenly.

"Oh," Suleka responded, remembering her mission. "Well, Detective Deller wants you to help with this missing woman case."

"A woman's gone missing?"

"You didn't hear about that?"

"You know I never hear about things around here."

"Usually, yes, but you went to the library today."

Lange was perplexed. "What's that got to do with anything?" Then he honed in one what interested him. "Who went missing?"

"Margery Breckenridge, though everyone calls her Margi. She and her husband, Sam, live over on the Rockport-Cascade Road. He was away for a few days and came home Sunday to find the house empty. But her car was in the driveway and her purse was on the counter in the kitchen where she always left it so he figured she couldn't be far. He waited and then when she didn't show by dinnertime he called some of the neighbors but nobody had seen her, so he waited some more. When she didn't show up by bedtime, he got worried and called the Sheriff."

"I'm guessing his wife doesn't carry a cell phone?"

"Well she does but it was in her purse...."

"...in the kitchen," finished Lange. He had more questions but he knew there wasn't any point in asking Suleka. She tended to have the bare bones of any story floating around the Upper Skagit but not more than that. Plus the accuracy of her information depended on who gave it to her. He suddenly noticed that he was cold, the October evening having penetrated his jacket, and his urge to get inside and start a fire in his woodstove grew. He pulled the cell phone away from his ear, to hang up, when he remembered something. "How did you know I went to the library today?"

"Britta told me you'd been in." Lange didn't say anything. "She works there."

"I know that."

"Well I'm never sure with you," Suleka countered. "Some people you acknowledge and some you don't."

Lange looked at the phone again and hung up, having already moved on in his mind to the next thing. He slipped it back in his pocket, pulled the zipper on his jacket clear up under his chin to keep his neck warm and lifted the wheelbarrow, pushing it through the rutted dirt towards his yurt. Now that the heating season was starting he'd have to blade this area of ground, he thought to himself, maybe even order some loads of gravel to make this journey with the wheelbarrow easier.

He reached the two steps leading up to the little platform outside his door and set the wheelbarrow down. He leaned forward and loaded his arms with firewood, then climbed the steps to his door. He nudged the handle down with his right elbow until it let him push the door open and walked into the round, canvas space. Even with the firewood in his arms, he made a beeline for the Pirateer game.

He leaned down, freed his right arm and moved one of his pirate ships three spaces down the trade winds and five spaces across the diagonal to take Suleka's ship with the gold. Done! He flipped the gold coin onto the thistle decal inside his ship and set Suleka's skull and crossbones decaled ship on the matching flag next to her harbor, so it was out of the game. He glanced at the clock over his bed and awkwardly scribbled down the time of his move on the piece of paper next to the game. He and Suleka played on the honor system and neither of them cheated. Now she would have 24 hours from the time she saw the board again until she had to make her move. Not that she would need it. Lange was always impressed with how quickly she made her moves - as if she could see the game and was always one step ahead of him. Fortunately that was only in Pirateer. He had a tendency to dominate every other game they played.

He crossed to the wood box and let the firewood tumble out of his arms into it, creating a series of rolling booms like thunder in the distance. He brushed the loose wood chips on the front of his jacket down into the box then stopped, narrowing his eyes and gently sucking on his retainer. Stealing beans and milk and a can opener suggested someone homeless and hungry. At least, in NYC he'd be looking for someone who fit that profile. Stealing his firewood fit too, especially since, as Suleka had said, the other thefts had happened not far from his property. The only thing was, he was sure there'd been more than one person at his place. So maybe it was a family, working to steal what they needed. But then why walk as far as his place for a couple of armloads of firewood?

Lange pushed his thumbs under the straps of his daypack and pulled it off his shoulders. The pack slipped down his arms. He caught it in his left hand and swung it onto the black leather footstool he had in front of its matching chair by the wood stove, thinking he'd empty the groceries out of it after he lit a fire. He'd been hoping to go up into the Pass tomorrow, do a little early season deer hunting but if Deller needed his help maybe he wouldn't. He crouched in front of the woodstove and picked up a starter brick of compressed sawdust, made from waste wood at the local guitar manufacturing business. He ran his thumb lightly over the outline of a guitar pressed into the top of the three-inch thick yellow oval, then slipped it into his woodstove. He snapped apart a small, wafer thin square of cedar kindling, leaned the pieces up against the guitar brick and searched the hearth for a sliver of pitch wood. He found one, pulled the lighter out of the pocket of his pants and flipped open the lid, intending to light the pitch wood, but then stopped. What made him think they'd walked? Maybe they'd driven up to his gate, left the vehicle and high tailed it in from there to grab what they wanted of his firewood. He made a phuhf of exasperation. Some people! A light glow was beginning to radiate across the skylight above him and he tipped his head towards it. It would be a full moon tonight.

Lange went back to the pitch wood. The resin on the fir was like gasoline the way it lit right up. He held the flame against the cedar and watched it lick around the thin sticks of deep brown until they caught. He dropped the pitch wood under the kindling and sat back on his heels. The flames grew, engulfing the cedar and making pockets of orange in the surface of the guitar brick as Lange balanced longer and larger lengths of wood on top. He wondered whether ownership of a vehicle was really in keeping with people who were homeless and hungry?

He also wondered whether any of this really mattered in light of somebody going missing? He closed the door to the firebox and stood up, watching the flames leap towards the wedges of fir on top. He heard the first loud snap of gas igniting and knew that his fire was well underway. He wanted to stand there longer, watching the lights flicker and grow, but he knew he had to go out, to where he had cell service, and call Deller back. He slipped his hand inside the pocket of his jacket and let his fingers touch his cell phone. Then he made a beeline for the door.

*****

He kept a utility flashlight sitting on a shelf next to the door, which he grabbed on his way out. As soon as he'd cleared the threshold, he felt the cold of the October evening again and hustled to stay ahead of it. He trotted down the steps and turned to the right, intending to head for the gate to his property where he knew he could get cell phone reception, but after just a few strides he remembered the spot between his firewood pile and his yurt where he'd received the call from Suleka. Why go all the way out to the gate if he didn't need to, he asked himself?

Lange abruptly turned to the right again and took a dozen steps towards his firewood. He switched the flashlight from his right hand to his left and pulled his cell phone out of his pocket. He looked for bars - nothing. He walked a few more paces - still nothing. He took his eyes off the phone and shone the flashlight over the ground to see if he could find the tracks from the wheelbarrow and stumbled on some bracken underfoot. He pitched clumsily sideways two steps, his right arm extending out reflexively as a counterbalance, and heard his cell phone chime, meaning he had a voicemail. He bounced immediately to the place where his hand had been and spied the service bars. He ignored the 2 voicemails indicated on the screen and dialed Deller's number from memory. She picked up instantly.

"Are you on your way?"

"On my way where?"

"Didn't you get my voicemails?"

Lange paused. "I just found service on my property."

"Meaning you didn't listen to them, right?"

He imagined she was giving him a piercing look with her dark brown eyes right now and squaring off her shoulders to discourage backtalk. "I thought it would be quicker just to call you."

There was a pause. Deller's tone was softer when she spoke

again and Lange knew that she'd remembered he was just a helper here and not one of her deputies. "I was hoping you'd come and take a look around the Breckenridge property." Lange didn't say anything. "I assume, you've heard about this?"

He hadn't said anything because he was wondering how much he could do at this hour. "Suleka gave me the basics but...it's dark."

"Not inside the house it isn't."

"But she didn't go missing inside the house."

"You sure about that?"

Lange's adrenaline spiked. "You're thinking something happened inside the house?"

"Well I'm not...."

"Why? What did you find?"

"It's not exactly what we found..."

"Are you there now? Can I come over?"

"I was hoping you would." Frankie Deller's tone was pointed and Lange ran quickly through all the possibilities why.

"Is the husband there right now?"

"Uh-huh."

"And you think he's involved?"

"Mmmmmmmm," hummed Deller, like maybe.

Lange didn't need to know more. He just needed to get started. "Can you text me the address?" he asked, heading for the door to his yurt. Then he remembered the spotty service on his property and pulled the phone away from his ear. Damn! Call failed. He rushed back to where he'd been standing and looked at his phone but the service indicator gave him no bars. He lifted the phone high above his head and moved it around. Still nothing. He reached the other way, down towards the ground and it rang. He thrust his right ear down to the phone, eager not to miss the call, and answered with his butt up in the air. "Yes?" he shouted, as if the level of his voice might make a difference to whether he kept the person on the line or not.

"You don't have to yell," said Deller. "I can hear you."

"Well I lost you there…."

"I gathered that."

Lange was irked that she wasn't picking up on his sense of urgency. "And I'm in kind of an awkward position…."

"Me too!" responded Deller and Lange knew she meant with the husband being there. "I'll text you the address but…"

"I'll ride my bike over."

"If you'll let me finish," insisted Deller and Lange bit down on his urge to tell her to hurry up before he got a crick in his back. "Suleka's on her way over to get you."

"She is?"

Almost as soon as he said it, Lange heard Suleka's Nissan chugging down his driveway towards him. He swiveled around to face her in his forward bend and instantly lost Deller again. He snapped himself upright but Suleka has already seen him with his butt in the air and called out the open window of her truck, "Well I'm not surprised you bark when you answer the telephone if you do it cramped over like that!"

Callum Lange twitched his lips, searching for a pithy reply, but when nothing came to mind he huffed, "Let me close the woodstove down and then we can leave."

Suleka was already half way out of the Nissan however. "We're not going anywhere till I've had a chance to look at that Pirateer board."

Lange was already on the move and flapped his hand dismissively. "We don't have time for that!"

"You don't maybe. But I do. I'm assuming you made your move."

"I did. But Deller made it sound urgent."

"That's okay. It won't take me but a second."

"You can't know that!" She'd caught up with him at the door to his yurt and he stood back, letting her pass in front of him.

"'S'nice and warm in here," she said, making straight for the game board. "What time did you get home?"

"I don't know. Ten minutes ago maybe." He strode across to his woodstove and threw another piece of wood on the small fire. Then he began the process of closing down all the drafts to keep the fire smoldering and to protect against a chimney fire.

"Your woodstove is pretty efficient to have got this place so toasty in ten minutes."

"It is but I also have the electric heaters running off the hydro." He tightened down the last of the drafts on the stove, straightened back up and turned around to find Suleka standing right behind him. "You made your move already?!"

She just smiled as he rushed back to the board. "Do you have groceries in this backpack?" She was pointing at the blue and grey daypack he'd deposited on the footstool.

"My ice cream!" Lange remembered.

"Don't worry, I'll get it." She flapped her hand at him as if he should go back to what he was doing. "Just don't spend too long looking at the board."

But the sixty-year old, ex-detective from NYC had already seen the move she'd made; she'd taken his thistle ship, got back the gold and was heading towards her harbor unimpeded. Damn! He took a big breath in, extending every inch of his six foot one frame, ballooned his chest, then deflated instantly, with a noisy huff of frustration. "I wish I knew what makes you so good at this," he griped.

Suleka pushed the almost melted ice cream into the back of the freezer, hoping it would solidify again, then flipped her long, dark braid over her shoulder and slipped her hands inside the front of her denim overalls to rest on her plump belly. "You've got to think like a pirate to catch a pirate."

"Whatever that means," he said, crossing the yurt to head out the door again.

Suleka ran her eyes around the circle of the yurt. "I don't see any electric heaters."

"They're under the floor."

"That's where the heat's coming from?" She stepped out of one of her muck boots and put her foot directly on the plywood floor. She giggled as she felt the warmth radiate through her green and yellow striped sock. "This is delicious," she told Lange.

He rolled his eyes even though he was pleased. He'd always wanted to live in a place with radiant floor heat and even though the yurt was only temporary, he'd decided to try it out. Especially since he'd found a way to have free electricity. "We really should get going," he told her.

She slipped her boot back on. "You know, the creek on my property is pretty steep." He stepped past her and opened the door. "Maybe you could show me how to make hydro-electricity."

"Maybe." He motioned for her to step outside and when she did, he closed the door behind her. Then he looked up at the sky. There were stars everywhere, shimmering in the night sky like sequins on a country singer's dress. He wondered whether the missing woman was somewhere in these mountains, looking up at these same stars.

"You coming?" Suleka asked.

He flipped around and saw her standing halfway between his yurt and her truck. He crossed the small platform outside his door in two strides and trotted down the steps. "This missing woman," he remarked as he came up alongside Suleka. "Why does Deller think the husband is involved?"

"Margi's husband?" They walked together the last few feet to the Nissan and broke apart to go to their respective doors. Suleka shrugged at Lange over the top of the cab. "Maybe because he's dating a twenty-three year old?"

Lange pushed his lips tighter together; that would explain it.

*****

Once they crossed the bridge over the Skagit River, Lange sat taller in his seat and leaned forward, wanting to see if he could somehow detect the homes that had been burglarized. "Were they along this stretch of the highway?" he asked Suleka.

A crease appeared in her brow. "What?"

"The houses that were broken into?"

"I think. Maybe." She shrugged. "I don't know."

"How come?"

"Well I didn't find out their names! You know how it is..." She circled her right hand in the air. "A friend told me."

Lange pounced. "Which friend?"

"Shari. She lives down here." Her face opened up with realization. "Not far from where we're going actually."

"Did she have something stolen from her too?"

"Who? Shari? No." She said it like she was sure but then her head swayed from side to side as if she were having second thoughts. "Well not exactly. Not like the others."

Lange wanted to press her for clarification but in the few months that Suleka had been working for him, buying his groceries, cleaning his yurt, driving him places and once helping him with a case, he'd learned that he was better off waiting for an explanation than asking for one. Tall spindly trees lined the highway to their right and even though it was dark, Lange used the beam from the headlights to count fifteen trees before Suleka continued.

"She didn't have anything tangible taken. What happened was Shari came home from the store last Wednesday...." She cocked her head to one side. "What day are we today?"

"Tuesday."

Suleka squinted, as if calculating something. "Then no, it was Thursday. She came home from the store last Thursday and when she took the groceries into her kitchen, she heard the dryer going in the mud room. So she thought Russ - her husband - must have got home early from his trip to the VA hospital, started some laundry, then gone out to the garage to work. He's rebuilding the transmission on their grandson's Toyota pick-up." Suleka paused and cocked her head to one side again. "Or is it a Chevy pick-up?"

Lange sighed and looked out the passenger window again, this time at a patch of scrubby wetland with spindly trees in the distance. This was going to take longer than he thought.

"Anyway, she unpacked all the groceries and went upstairs to do something on her computer and a little while later, she looked out the window by her desk and saw someone walking across her backyard." She paused, then blurted, "In their *underwear!*"

Lange knew that she expected him to be surprised so he dutifully spiked an eyebrow when she glanced at him even though, in his time in NYC, he'd seen a lot worse than people running around in their underwear.

Suleka snorted a little laugh. "Crazy, huh?"

Lange nodded.

"Anyway, as soon as she saw this Shari went tearing downstairs to get her husband, but once she got to the kitchen she could see this person through one of the windows going into her mud room. She put two and two together and figured out that Russ wasn't home – it was *this* guy doing *his* laundry in *her* mud room!!"

"Was it a guy?"

Suleka looked startled by the question. "I assume it was. She didn't say otherwise."

"Did she get a good look at him?"

"He was in his skivvies so I'm guessing yes."

"Guessing?!"

"Do you want to hear the rest of the story or not?!"

"Go on," he sighed.

But his interruption had caused Suleka to lose her train of thought. "Where was I?"

"She realized her husband wasn't home...,"

"Oh yes." The Nissan arced to the left, turning onto the Rockport-Cascade Road, and sped up. "She realized her husband wasn't home so she thought maybe instead of just going and confronting this guy – this *person*, sorry – she ought to get her Smith and Wesson semi-automatic. So she went back up to her bedroom, because that's where she keeps it, but by the time she got the pistol loaded and went back down to the mud room, the freeloading launderer was gone. So, you see," Suleka explained, "he stole time in Shari's washing machine but not her food or anything like that."

"I wish we could be sure it was a man."

"Why? What difference does that make?"

"It could have been the missing woman."

"Margi?! No. Shari said the person had long, straight dark hair and Margi's is short, curly and greyish. Plus why would she wash her clothes at Shari's when her place is not half a mile away?"

Lange didn't really know. It was just an idea on his part. He shrugged. "Like you said, people do crazy things."

"But Shari would have recognized Margi." Suleka braked as the Nissan approached Illabot Creek, and indicated to turn right, into a driveway, all the time looking at Lange. "Wouldn't she?"

Lange sat forward again. "Is this the place?" he asked.

Suleka nodded. "Sam and Margi's place, yes."

The headlights of the car shone on a cabin with a steeply sloping shed roof covered in grey sheet metal that almost matched the weathered grey of the shingled walls. It didn't look dilapidated so much as lived in. And loved. Suleka drove the Nissan down a narrow driveway lined with smooth river rock. Lange could see well-tended planter boxes at the base of the house, glass chimes and dried flowers hanging from the eaves, and gourds of varying colors and sizes grouped around the front steps. It was October, after all, he told himself; the season for squash on the steps.

A sleek, silvery Crown Victoria with Sheriff emblazoned on the side looked markedly out of place parked next to a row of firewood.

This obviously bothered the resident Chihuahua, who kept charging the car from the steps leading up to the deck, yapping ferociously, then scurrying back with a few bug-eyed glances over its shoulder. Suleka wanted to avoid crushing the tiny dog so she pulled up almost at the end of the driveway and switched off the Nissan.

In one swift move, Lange got out. He could see Deller's back through one of the downstairs windows, her dark ponytail swishing across the shoulders of her navy blue jacket as she shook her head from side to side. He slammed the door to the Nissan shut, thinking she'd turn and acknowledge his arrival, but instead she walked away from the window and slowly disappeared into the well-lit interior.

He moved away from the Nissan, towards some painted rocks sitting at the base of the planter boxes. They had large, brightly colored, 3D looking spots on them that gave the effect of beads in blown glass. It was a simple enough design but very eye catching. And strangely appealing, Lange thought.

"Watch out!" Suleka shouted across to him.

"What?" he cried and looked down to see his left foot almost crush the Chihuahua. He performed an off-balance dance around the pup, who continued its race, unperturbed, across the gravel to the steps, then promptly turned around and began charging the Sheriff's vehicle again. Lange stepped back, to give the dog an uninterrupted run.

"I don't know why I stopped you now that I think about it," Suleka confessed, as she walked towards Lange, letting the Chihuahua pass in front of her. "I've never liked that dog."

"Whose dog is it?"

"Margi's. She thinks the world of that mutt. Takes her everywhere."

Lange's piecing blue eyes narrowed. "And yet the dog's here and she's not."

"Yeah. I'd say she didn't leave voluntarily."

Lange nodded, already glad Suleka had come with him. He

lowered his voice. "Does anything else strike you as being wrong?"

Her brown eyes darted left and right behind her glasses as she became drawn into the act of detection. They settled on a simple pole building that was blocked by the Sheriff's car. "Her bicycle's here," she said.

"Which means....?"

"Well Margi always rides her bicycle when she goes out wildcrafting."

"Wildcrafting?"

Suleka splayed both hands out, palms up, in front of her. "She likes making art with things she finds in the woods." She nodded up at the porch. "Like the dried flower arrangements. And she makes bird feeders out of fir cones, and paints on those mushroom looking things that grow on the sides of trees. You know, the ones with the pale tops and dark bottoms. What are those called?"

"Conks."

"That's right. Conks. So if her bicycle's here, I'm thinking she didn't go missing because she got lost on one of her wildcrafting trips."

"She always travels by bike?"

"To go wildcrafting, yes. At least, that's what she told me. And Coco - " She pointed down at the dog. " - rides along in the basket on the front."

Lange nodded again.

The Chihuahua ran between them again, on her way back to the steps, and Lange watched, then followed, with Suleka tagging along behind. At the bottom of the steps they both made way for the dog to do an about turn before climbing up to the porch that ran the width of the cabin. An array of gourds with block, geometric designs painted on them and tiny, orange lights strung through them, lit the way to the door. Lange took in the basket of apples, the corn stalk scarecrow, the painted, wooden 'Welcome' sign and the threadbare armchair with a knitted, multi-colored blanket thrown over the back.

On a table, to one side of the armchair, a yellow butternut squash had been cut into and part of its soft interior emptied onto some newspaper. The squash had obviously been there a while because the moisture had dried on the newspaper, causing it to curl and buckle. Lange found the entire, half-finished mess at odds with everything else on the porch and was looking around for the knife that had been used to cut into the squash, when the door to the cabin opened.

Frankie Deller stood in the doorway, smartly dressed in a navy blue pantsuit, her Glock in its usual place on her hip. She nodded him in. Without saying anything Lange stepped over the threshold, looked back at Suleka and nodded her in too. He glanced beyond her again, still trying to spot the knife, but gave up as soon as he heard Deller start the introductions.

"This is Callum Lange, the detective I was telling you about, Mr. Breckenridge."

The downstairs of the cabin was open plan, with a small kitchen immediately to the right and a short wall between it and the rest of the downstairs. A kitchen table sat at the end of the wall, between the door and the living area, and beyond that Lange could see a woodstove in the far left corner of the cabin. A gaunt, grey-skinned, older man sitting on the right side of the table, with his back to the kitchen, threw an acid look in Suleka's direction. "Where's my wife?" he demanded.

"I have no idea, Sam." She stepped past Lange to be closer to him.

He curled his lips, bitter. "She'd better turn up soon before I get arrested for something I never done."

He slumped forward, wrapping his long-fingered hands around a coffee cup on the table in front of him, and Lange saw the sadness in the slump of his shoulders. "When did you last see her, Mr. Breckenridge?"

"Thursday morning," he growled. "I been over this already with *her*." He pointed a gnarly finger at Detective Deller, who had moved to a spot at the far end of the kitchen table, with her back to the living room. To her left, Lange could see a photograph pinned to the wall, next to a calendar, underneath a cream, wall mount, Trimline telephone. He took a step towards it and stared at a slightly younger Sam Breckenridge, his arm slung casually around a short, slight, curly haired woman. "Is this Margi?" he asked, pointing at the photo.

He heard Breckenridge grunt behind him. "Uh-huh."

"And she didn't tell you if she was going somewhere special? Or somewhere different?"

"No! How many times I gotta say it. No! She never tells me where she goes when I'm away and I don't ask."

Lange turned around to face him. "I'm only thinking if she knew she was going away for a few days, to visit a friend or a relative, she might have mentioned it."

Breckenridge relaxed a little with the friendliness in Lange's tone. He leaned back in his chair and let his arms hang down on either side of him. "Well she didn't. She wouldn't have wanted to spend overnight at a friend's house 'cause nobody likes that dog 'cept her. And she don't have any relatives live around here."

He looked up and there was a blankness in his gaze that made Lange think he didn't have the guile to lie. "Was she depressed?"

Breckenridge slumped forward again, looking sullen. "Why do people keep asking me that?"

Lange glanced at Deller; she lifted her eyebrows as if to say, go ahead, but Suleka beat him to it. She stepped forward and touched the husband lightly on his shoulder. "She might have killed herself, Sam."

Breckenridge looked blank again. "Why would she do that?"

Lange had seen something behind Breckenridge, on a shelf just above his head. He came around behind Suleka to take a closer look just as Deller said, "You are having an affair with a much younger woman." Lange stopped and focused on Breckenridge.

The man looked genuinely confused. "That's what you're

worried about? Margi don't give two hoots about that!" He looked at Suleka. "Does she?"

"Well I don't know," Suleka said, like this was a question she hadn't contemplated before. "She's never said anything to me."

"We've been married a long time," Sam went on, talking directly to Lange. "And I've always messed around on her. She knows that. She told me long as I don't leave her, she don't care." He sat up straighter. "We're happy enough. She's a good cook. And she keeps the place tidy." He said both like they were terms of his wife's employment and Lange could imagine Deller and Suleka biting down on some salty repartees. "No, I've said from the start, I think she went off on one of her gathering trips and took a fall."

"But her..." Suleka started but Lange nudged her back with his elbow a couple of times. She took the cue and shut up.

"Can I look around?" Lange asked.

"I guess," moped Breckenridge. Then pointed at Deller again. "Although she already did that so I doubt you'll find anything."

Lange looked across at Deller, who made sure the husband was focused on his coffee again before she blinked her dark eyes towards the kitchen area. The ex-detective swiveled around and took in the bay window overlooking the deck with a basket full of fall foliage sitting on the wide, white-tiled sill, the sink perpendicular to the window, with cabinets above and below, and the fridge to the left of the sink, opposite the window. His blue eyes honed in on what Deller must have been pointing him towards; the dark, round, nickel-sized stains on the floor mat in front of the sink. They were pretty well hidden in the pattern of sunflowers but after the years he'd spent on the job in NYC, finding them was like muscle memory for Lange. Of course, they could have been there for a while. He let his eyes trace back, from the mat, past the dog dishes on the floor under the window, to the front door; no more stains. He stepped over to the sink. There were a couple of dirty mugs and plates, a greasy skillet, a pot that looked like it had dried oatmeal in it, a bowl, a few utensils, evidence of the two days Margi hadn't been around to clean up after her husband, but Lange's trained eye caught a smear of dark red-brown where the sink met the counter in front of him. He kept searching and saw three, tiny, brownish splatters on the underside of the faucet and a big splotch on the black splash to the left of the sink. He began to picture Margi being stabbed in the neck with the knife she'd used to carve the pumpkin. He waited to see if he heard anything from the missing woman but it was quiet over by the sink. Quiet with a feeling of sadness.

Lange backed up a step and lifted a curtain under the sink. The garbage was there, exactly as he'd thought it would be. He tipped it towards him. There was an empty, family size chip bag on the top, which he lifted gingerly. "Bingo!" he whispered.

*****

Callum Lange glanced over his shoulder and caught Suleka's eye. "I need a bag," he mouthed, hoping to keep it between them.

She threw an awkward look at the others before moving towards him and Lange heard Deller's shoes tapping over the wood floor. "Did you find something?" she said.

"What?" came Breckenridge's voice, followed by the sound of a chair scraping across the floor.

Lange sighed. So much for doing this without an audience. Suleka peered over his shoulder and he watched her mouth drop open and her head pull back at the sight of the knife. "Is that blood?" she asked, obviously perturbed.

Before he could answer Deller shouldered past Suleka and held an evidence bag down close to the trash. "Here. Put it in this."

Lange leaned forward to oblige when a thought fluttered into his mind then back out before he could catch it. Damn, he hated when that happened. He was missing something, but what? It was something that he'd seen, something nearby. He suddenly felt crowded in the tiny kitchen and contemplated dumping the trash and legging it out to the porch, where he could look up at the moon and refocus his inner lens. Where the chill of the night air would inject some clarity into his thinking. But Breckenridge interrupted his escape plan. "You found the knife, huh."

The two detectives turned and looked at the man, saying nothing so he might incriminate himself further. Unfortunately Suleka hadn't been trained in the art of keeping her mouth shut. "You knew about this?" she balked, pointing at the knife.

"Yeah. I found it in the sink and I figured Margi cut herself."

"You didn't think it might be evidence?"

"Yeah, I did. But I didn't want the cops thinking it was evidence I stabbed her or something," he said, thrusting his chin forward, belligerent.

Lange blinked at the man. Now that Breckenridge was standing he didn't look as old as he had when slumped over in the kitchen chair. He was maybe 50, tall and angular, with the start of jowls on his jaw line and artificially darkened, slicked-down hair. Lange couldn't figure out if he was truly as transparent as he sounded or just a great liar. He blinked again and saw Deller watching him. She obviously couldn't make this guy out either.

"Was it the only thing in the sink, Mr. Breckenridge?" Lange asked.

"Uh-uh, no. It was under Margi's oatmeal bowl. I guess she didn't clean one of the mornings after breakfast." Breckenridge looked out the window next to him as if hoping to see her out in the dark there. "She does that sometimes; gets so involved in one of her craft projects she gets behind."

"Would she leave the dishes for days?"

Breckeridge shook his head. "Never. She never went to bed with dirty dishes in the sink."

So one day, in the last week, she'd had breakfast and hadn't been home to clean up, thought Lange. But which day?

"When did you find the knife in the sink?" Deller asked.

"Today," Breckenridge answered. "I wanted to make nachos for lunch so I was looking in the sink for the cheese grater."

Lange's mind went instantly to fingerprints. "And you felt it?"

"No, I saw it! Blood an' all."

"And you just picked it up and threw it in the trash?"

Breckenridge's jaw jutted forward again. "I picked it up with that sponge Margi uses to wash the dishes." They all stared at him. "Hey, I didn't want to touch it! Not with the blood on it. Plus your deputy," - he looked at Deller – "The one that came and talked to me? He'd already given me the stink eye, like he suspected me of doing something bad to Margi, so I wasn't gonna put my prints on the knife."

Lange had had enough. He tipped the knife into the evidence bag, let go of the trash and squared off in front of Breckenridge. "If you find anything else that you think might be useful to us, please leave it alone."

Then he marched outside and stood for a moment on the deck, looking up at the gloriously incandescent harvest moon. What is it I'm not seeing? he thought, frustrated. Deller came out to stand beside him. She placed the knife in the evidence bag on the porch rail in front of them. "A sponge!" she scoffed. "So much for prints."

Lange grunted.

"Maybe he's smarter than he seems."

"Permit me to doubt! Although I think he's right; she cut herself, maybe when she was carving that gourd." He nodded towards the butternut squash on the porch table. "And she ran to the kitchen sink to clean up." He looked up at the moon again, chewing on his dentures while he thought. "Whatever happened, it was the last thing that happened before she went missing."

"If she *is* missing."

"If she is missing," Lange agreed.

"You think the cut was bad enough she went to the Emergency

Room and something happened from there?"

"Then why would her car be here?"

A skittering to their left caused them to turn. The Chihuahua was at the top of the porch steps, head tipped back, glaring at them like they shouldn't be there. They waited, in full stand-off mode, then watched the little creature race across the porch, trying to avoid eye contact while constantly glancing at them, and dart in through the partially open door behind them. Lange reached back and closed the door behind the dog. "Tell me what you know," he said.

Deller slipped her hands in her pants pockets, flapping her elbows out. "Not that much," she confessed. "Breckenridge called us on Sunday night and spoke with a deputy, who told him to wait overnight since it was late and there was no real timeline on when Margi may have gone missing, if she had gone missing. Breckenridge called back early the next morning and our dispatcher said he was agitated - borderline abusive - like he was really worried. So Deputy Collins drove up here to follow up."

Lange snorted and the sound ricocheted off the trees around the cabin. Deller got defensive. "Hey, Collins may not be fast but he's thorough."

Lange didn't press it. "Go on."

"With Margi's car and purse being left here, Collins was initially concerned; but then he found out from Breckenridge that there's a Women's Retreat up at Baker Lake, which Margi had talked about going to. It started last Saturday and goes till tomorrow, and Breckenridge said if she had gone, it was almost certain that one of her friends would have driven her."

"He didn't call to see if his wife was there?"

"There's no cell phone service that far up the mountain."

"Oh." Lange chewed on this. "So Collins drove up there."

Deller nodded. "He did. But no Margi. Her friend was there and said that Margi hadn't gone along because all the fall colors were out and she wanted to get some boughs and leaves for her craft projects.

I guess she makes items that she sells at holiday fairs. Does pretty well from them too. Collins came back down and shared this information with Breckenridge who got worked up all over again because this was what he'd been saying from the start; that Margi had gone out gathering and maybe taken a fall. And he told Collins that if she'd gone wildcrafting over by Lake Caskey, which she did a lot, then what if she'd fallen into the lake? Although now that I say that, I think he may have been blowing smoke because he told us both that he didn't know where Margi went gathering."

"And he *didn't* tell anyone that she always went gathering on her bicycle, in which case, why is it here in the shed?"

Deller's dark eyes flashed anger. "Collins obviously thought Lake Caskey was a lead," she went on, "because he called Search and Rescue. Turns out they were up Illabot Creek, looking for a missing hiker. They found the guy and he was fine, he'd just lost the trail and hunkered down overnight, but as a result they didn't respond to Collins' request till this morning. And then they spent a good chunk of time walking the woods around the lake, but didn't find anything."

"Why did they search Lake Caskey if there was no car in the area to suggest Margi was there?"

Deller's eyes flashed again. "They were looking for a bike."

"So Breckenridge *did* tell him she traveled by bike?"

"Yep."

"And Collins didn't see the bike was here?!"

A coyote yipped a half a dozen times further up the Cascade but Lange kept staring at Deller. He saw her cheeks flex and knew she was biting down on her anger – whether at him or at Collins he didn't know and didn't give a damn – then her shoulders slumped in resignation. "Apparently not."

Lange stormed to the end of the porch. This was a mess! Badly handled from the get go. "Why didn't you call me in sooner?" he barked.

Deller marched after him. "Hey, I wasn't called in myself until just this afternoon and that was after Collins came back here and found out from the neighbors that Breckenridge has a girlfriend. A very young girlfriend!"

Lange looked off into the distance, at the inky black silhouettes of the trees against the softly lit sky. Somewhere out there was a person of interest eating canned goods pilfered from homes in the neighborhood, and a woman without her dog. Her dog! Immediately Lange caught the thought that had eluded him, swung around and marched back into the cabin, Deller behind him. Suleka was sitting opposite Breckenridge at the kitchen table, talking softly with him. "Was the dog inside when you got home, Mr. Breckenridge?"

"Uh-huh, yep."

"And was there food in the dog bowl?"

Breckenridge became defensive. "I fed her!"

"I'm sure you did," soothed Lange. "I'm just curious if the bowl was empty when you put more out?"

"Yeah, mostly. Except for what she'd spilled out onto the floor. That's what made me think to feed her. I thought Margi would have a fit if she saw that mess so I scooped it up and dumped it back in her bowl."

"And the dog ate?"

"Nope. Wasn't hungry then, I guess." He looked over at the tiny pup, chowing down on the dry dog food in her bowl as they spoke.

"Does she often spill her food out onto the floor?"

"No. Not usually. She's very tidy. And Margi's tidy when she feeds her." He shrugged. "I guess she was agitated, with Margi not being here. Dogs do that, huh?"

Lange contemplated this for a moment before going on. "Did Margi ever walk out into the woods close by the house for her wildcrafting activities?"

Irritation flicked across Breckenridge's face. "Maybe. I don't know for sure. All I know is I'd come home to baskets of leaves and twigs and ferns and crap like that on the kitchen table. Sometimes she'd tell me where they came from; sometimes not. Does it matter?"

"I'm just trying to figure out why Margi left her dog behind if she went out gathering."

The husband's eyes grew bigger and his face filled with consternation as he looked across at the dog again and Lange couldn't tell if it was because he'd forgotten that detail when plotting his wife's disappearance or because he was now truly scared that something bad had happened to Margi.

Suleka must have assumed the later because she leaned across the table and forced him to make eye contact with her. "We'll find her, Sam. We'll find her."

*****

The last thing Lange examined before he left the Breckenridge home was the painted gourd he'd seen sitting on the shelf above the kitchen table. He'd moved to take a closer look earlier, but had been interrupted by the talk of Breckenridge's infidelities. The gourd, however, continued to catch his eye. It was an acorn squash, turned into a canvas for a painting of a black bear walking through the woods. It was cleverly executed with the ridges on the gourd giving depth to the trees that were acting as camouflage for the bear. It wasn't the kind of art that Lange usually liked but he liked this one. "Did Margi paint this?" he asked.

Breckenridge craned his head around and looked up. "Yep," he grunted. "And it's mine."

"I wasn't going to...."

"Lot of people have tried to buy that one," he went on, overriding Lange. "But Margi gave it to me."

"You know, I saw that up there," said Suleka, gazing up at the gourd, "but I didn't think it was Margi's. I've only ever seen the ones she does with the colors on them. Like the ones on the porch."

"First time she tried wildlife," boasted Breckenridge, "and everyone says how good it is. I had somebody offer me four hundred bucks for that one."

Lange had been about to touch the gourd but changed his mind. He spun around and pulled both sides of his mouth down at Deller, impressed. She flexed her eyebrows back at him as if to say, "I told you."

"Your wife's obviously got talent," Lange remarked.

"Yeah she does. You should see the new ones."

Lange narrowed his eyes, curious.

Breckenridge went on. "When Margi saw how much people liked the bear, she did others; a deer, a bald eagle, a coyote with its cub – a whole bunch of different ones." He paused and Lange could almost see the images running through his mind. "The one with the wolves is my favorite. I bet she sells that for a ton of money."

Suleka perked up in her seat. "Can we see them?"

"I don't know where they are," Sam Breckenridge said, looking around. "She had about eight or nine of them in a big fruit box, here on the kitchen table."

"You think they're missing?" asked Lange.

"Nah. She probably moved them out to the backseat of her car already, ready to take to a shop, or a fair. Something like that."

Thinking of the rash of burglaries close by, Lange pressed it. "Have you noticed anything else missing from your house, Mr. Breckenridge? Anything at all?"

"Just my wife," he replied with an edge of surliness. But the lines in his face got heavy with sadness as he looked up at Lange. "Ain't that enough?"

*****

Lange strode back across the porch, down the steps and

crunched across the gravel driveway, leading Deller and Suleka to a point far enough away from the cabin to ensure privacy. The temperature had dropped to a biting near freezing and when he spun to face the women he noticed that they huddled in close to him, without touching, as if proximity might bring them some warmth.

"What are you thinking?" Deller asked with a nod in his direction.

"I'm thinking thirty-six hundred dollars is a lot of money to find sitting on the kitchen table."

"The petty thief moved on to bigger things?" asked Suleka.

"What petty thief?" The gap between Deller's eyebrows narrowed.

"You haven't heard about that?"

"You can explain in a minute," Lange jumped in, impatient to keep moving forward. He looked at Deller. "Do you know if the friend up at the Women's Retreat stopped by to find out if Margi wanted to go, or just called?"

"No idea. I could hook you up with Collins but he's questioning the girlfriend right now."

"That's okay. I should go talk to this woman anyway. D'you have her name?"

Deller pulled a small, red, spiral-bound notepad out of her jacket pocket and flipped through the pages, trying to beat the cold by going fast. "Mary Lynn McCracken," she read.

"You know her?" Lange was looking at Suleka, who sank further down into the black knit scarf around her neck. Around them downed branches and limbs were already popsicle white with hoar frost and everything was quiet in a way Lange had never experienced in New York.

"Uh-huh. Not very well though. You think she might have seen something?"

"She might," said Lange as he moved away, his mind leapfrogging over to the possibility of the gourds in the back of

Margi's car. He saw a Toyota pick-up that he assumed belonged to Sam Breckenridge, parked perpendicular to Deller's Crown Victoria and a white, Subaru station wagon parked in the shed. That was probably Margi's. He walked towards it, using the light from the moon to scour the ground for signs. Signs of what, he wasn't sure, but he had a sense that there had to be something that might point him in Margi's direction.

The ground revealed nothing and Lange gave Margi's yellow Schwinn bicycle, which was leaning up against the outside of the shed, a quick once over with his eyes, but saw nothing out of the ordinary there either. Behind him he heard Suleka recounting details of the local burglaries to Deller, her voice echoing out into the trees in the quiet of the evening. He slipped inside the shed to check the Subaru. He flipped his phone out of his pocket and activated the flashlight app. A bright beam of light shone on the back seat of the Subaru where Lange saw nothing other than a small pet carrier. A deep hmmm vibrated in his throat. Where was the fruit box full of painted gourds?

He ran the flashlight over the front seats and the floor of the station wagon and then walked around to the back of the vehicle. He squeezed the handle on the hatch back with the fingers of his left hand and it popped open, allowing him to run the flashlight over the floor. But there was nothing more than a few stray boughs, a leash for the dog and a couple of cloth shopping bags. He let the hatch back fall closed and stood for a moment, sucking softly on the plate in the roof of his mouth. He turned 180 degrees, letting his gaze blur in the dark on the other side of the cabin. He was supposed to find something out here, he was sure of it, but he couldn't figure out what.

Lange became aware that Deller and Suleka had stopped talking and were watching him from where he'd left them standing in the middle of the driveway. He didn't want to make them stand in the cold any longer than necessary, especially since it didn't seem that there was anything worth finding out here. But then he noticed that the women weren't the only ones watching him. Coco was sitting at the top of the porch steps, staring at him with her big, round eyes. She was very intent, as if willing him to find something, and her posture caused Lange to crouch down, close to the ground, and shine his flashlight under the Crown Victoria. Yep, there was something under there, too far away to reach, but something small and white, alongside a hunk of vine maple.

He stood back up, feeling an excited thrum in his chest. "Frankie, move your vehicle, would you."

"You see something?" she asked as she crossed towards her car.

"Something," he nodded, "but I don't know that it's anything. Just back up a few feet."

Deller didn't argue. She slipped into the driver's seat, turned the engine on and eased the vehicle back half a car length. Lange saw what he'd been looking at under the car and held up his hand for her to stop. He stepped towards the small, white item and heard, before he saw, Coco racing across the gravel to get there ahead of him. "Stop that dog!" he yelled, fearing the tiny Chihuahua would chew the evidence before he'd even had a chance to examine it. Suleka lunged, Deller sprinted and Lange lurched forward but they weren't fast enough. Coco had the length of vine maple in her jaw and was dragging it across the gravel, growling at them to leave her alone.

"Oh *that's* what she wanted," Suleka remarked and looked at Deller. "No wonder she kept charging your car. You parked on her toy."

Lange was squatting over the ground by where the dog had retrieved the vine maple. "Fortunately that's not what I was after," he muttered, his eyes on a small rectangle of white paper with a hole in one end. It looked like someone had written something on the paper but it had obviously been stepped on and rained on so the markings were smeared and hard to decipher. Deller was peering over Lange's shoulder. "What is that?" she asked. "A price tag?"

Lange blinked and pulled his head back, looking at the rectangle differently. "Oh now that could be," he said. He pulled a Leatherman tool out of the pocket of his jeans and used the scissor attachment to gently lift the paper up off the ground. Detective Deller was ready with another evidence bag. "D'you carry those around in your pocket?" Lange asked, as he dropped the paper into the bag.

"Always," she answered.

Suleka was peering at the ground next to Coco. "I think I've found something else," she said.

Lange crab walked over to her, shining his flashlight on the ground to be sure he didn't step on anything important and saw what Suleka had discovered. It was a cluster of small, opaque pearls on inch long lengths of twine. He fished around in the gravel with the scissors to expose them and found they were being held together by a figure eight clasp on silver hook. "An earring," he said as he lifted it up into the air.

He heard Suleka suck in a short breath of air. "That's Margi's," she said.

"It doesn't mean anything," he reassured her as he stood up, "other than she lost her earring on the ground here."

"But you're going to put it in an evidence bag."

"I am," he nodded, feeling suddenly tired. Why did he always have to be the one to cause the hope to cloud in people's eyes? He offered Suleka a half smile and swiveled, expecting to see another evidence bag, but the Skagit County Sheriff's Detective's attention was on the dog.

Callum followed her gaze and saw the little pup sniffing slowly, methodically, at the moss on one end of the branch, her right paw intermittently popping up to touch at it, as if to release more of the scents contained within it. "What are you thinking?" he asked Deller.

"I'm thinking that's not a toy," she said and glanced up at Lange for corroboration. He nodded.

"Nooooo!" Suleka argued as she realized what they were

implying.

Deller said nothing. She pulled a latex glove out of the other pocket of her jacket stretched it over the fingers of her right hand and bent towards the vine maple. Coco bared her teeth and snapped but Deller wasn't intimidated. She grabbed the stick in one swift move and marched it over to her car, the pup racing at her feet the whole way, yapping and jumping in frustration.

"We're detectives, Suleka," Lange said. "We're trained to think the worst."

"Somebody could have peed on that stick and that dog would take an interest," she snorted back.

"That could be," he agreed. "But we don't have much to go on here."

Deller marched back towards them, leaving Coco scrabbling at the passenger side door of the Crown Victoria, obviously wishing for the reappearance of the vine maple. The Sheriff's detective held out another bag and Suleka watched as Lange dropped the earring down into it. "What's next?" he asked once the evidence was secured.

"I want to take these items to the lab and see what, if anything, has been written up on this....what did you call him?" she asked Suleka.

"The man in the mud room."

"Yeah. That guy. It could be nobody's filed a report because the thefts were so minor but I'll check."

Lange opened his mouth to speak and then thought better of it. He turned his focus on Suleka. "D'you think you can you find out who exactly has complained of things missing from their places around here?"

"I'm sure I could," Suleka replied slowly, thinking about it. Then she did a double take in his direction. "You mean tonight?"

Lange nodded. "I'd appreciate it. If we get it narrowed down to a certain area, we might be able to use the Search and Rescue dogs to try to track the thief."

Deller shook her head no. "I'll be using them to track Margi."

"That might amount to the same thing," said Lange.

There was a pause, while they all digested this thought. The coyote yipped again, the sound rounder, more resonant, closer than before and Coco gave up on the vine maple and hurried back to the cabin.

"What are you going to do?" Deller asked of Lange.

"I'm going to interview Mary Lynn McCracken."

"Again, *tonight*?!" Suleka repeated.

"There's plenty of time," countered Lange. "It's what, five o'clock?"

"Can't be." Suleka pulled the pocket watch she'd inherited from her father out of her jacket. "I didn't pick you up until after five so it's got to be..." She glanced at the face. "Well it's almost six-thirty."

"If Mary Lynn McCracken did come here on Saturday she might tell us something, even something random, that could point us in Margi's direction," Lange reasoned. He watched Suleka stare at him from behind her glasses and he could tell from the far away look in her brown eyes that she was vacillating. "Before it's too late," he added.

She relented but not entirely. "Couldn't you at least call Collins first?" she asked. "Find out if he knows whether she was here before we go trekking all the way up to Baker Lake?"

"No need," said Deller, looking over Lange's shoulder towards the Rockport-Cascade Road. "He's here."

They turned and squinted into a pair of headlights easing towards them down the narrow driveway. It was Collins in the Ford Expedition. He stopped the vehicle about thirty feet away from them, killed the engine and climbed down, carefully latching the door behind him. He stepped solidly towards them, his stocky frame bulked out in his dark green, winter uniform, the nasal whine in his breathing overriding the sound of his footsteps on the gravel.

"Did you bring dinner?" Deller asked. Collins' heavy breathing stopped as he hesitated, mid-stride, with a deer-in-the-headlights kind of look at his boss. "Kidding," she said, without even a hint of a smile. "What did you find out?"

Collins continued forward until he reached their huddle. "Not much," he said, with a sideways glance in Lange's direction. He pulled a spiral notebook like Deller's out of his jacket pocket, flipped past the Miranda rights card he had clipped on the inside of the front cover, and continued through the pages till he found what he was looking for. His eyes settled on an entry and Lange couldn't tell if he was just trying to avoid further eye contact or if he was really reading what he'd written. "Breckenridge picked up his girlfriend, Shelby, at her house Thursday morning to go on this camping trip with him east of the mountains and dropped her off Sunday afternoon, just before he came back here. She didn't seem too concerned that Margi wasn't here. She said Sam told her Margi's been a bit out of it lately."

"Out of it how?" asked Lange.

"I asked the same thing," said Collins, still with his eyes on his notebook. "But she didn't give me much of an answer. She said things like moody, spacey, difficult but she couldn't give me any examples. I got the impression she doesn't think much of Margi but I'm pretty sure she doesn't think much of anybody." He flicked his blue eyes up at Deller. "Except herself."

"Did Breckenridge say anything to you about Margi being different recently?" Lange asked Deller. She shook her head no. He turned the question, unspoken, on Suleka, who popped her nose and mouth out of her wool scarf to answer. "She has been a bit withdrawn but I thought it was because she was busy wildcrafting."

"Did Shelby give you any ideas as to where Margi might be?" Deller asked Collins.

"Didn't know and didn't care," he stated.

"So you think she's not involved?"

"I wouldn't go that far," Collins said. "Not yet anyway. She didn't seem to care if Margi was found which made me wonder if she had a hand in her not being around. But if she is involved, it would have to be with the husband because they were together the whole weekend."

"Or so they say," Lange added.

"They camped with friends. I'm on my way to question the friends now."

Deller looked perplexed. "Why d'you come back here?"

"To get Margi's cell phone."

"It's in my car," Deller tipped her head towards the Crown Victoria. "I was going to have someone call the last numbers Margi called. See if she said anything that might lead us to her."

"Me too," said Collins.

"Go right ahead," Deller encouraged. "It's in with the evidence bags."

"Does anyone know when Margi used her cell phone last?" Lange asked.

"Friday night. I checked the first time I came out here," Collins replied. He flipped through the pages of his notebook again and this time it was obvious he was reading his notes. "She called someone Friday, at 9:04 in the evening, and missed a call Saturday morning, at 8:11."

"That was probably this Mary Lynn McCracken," Deller said to Lange, "calling to see if Margi was going up to the retreat."

"Mmmm no," said Collins. "Her story was she told Margi to call her if she wanted to go and when she didn't get a call by 8:00 am on Saturday, she took off without her."

"And without coming by here," Lange pondered aloud.

Collins looked up from his notes to make eye contact with Lange. "She got kind of weepy saying she hoped nothing bad had happened to Margi because she'd feel terrible for not stopping by if that was the case."

There was another moment of quiet and then Suleka interrupted it by making a move. "I'm going home," she announced, trudging determinedly towards her pick-up. "I'll give you a ride if you want, Callum, but you'll have to come now. I don't want to call people too late to ask about the robberies around here and I want to have something to eat before I start."

"Go ahead," Frankie Deller said to Lange and followed Suleka's cue by walking towards her own vehicle. Collins got in step behind her and suddenly Lange was alone in the middle of the driveway. "There's nothing more we can do here tonight," he heard Frankie call out to him before opening a door on the Crown Victoria.

But there was one more thing Lange thought he could do; he could wait for the sound of Margi to come to him. He tipped his chin up and let his blue eyes circle the silence in the night sky, waiting for the noises he knew he should hear if he were to solve this case. When nothing came he made himself focus on the diminutive, mousy haired woman with the shy smile he'd seen in the photograph; the black bear that she'd painted; the sheen of the animal's thick coat captured in the light coming through the trees. Lange waited, expecting a noise in his aura to suggest that whatever had happened, it had been against Margi's will. But as much as he strained, all he could hear was Deller and Collins talking low a few feet away from him.

He sighed. Maybe Margi *had* just walked into the woods on one of her gathering mission and fallen into an unexpected grave. He heard Suleka start the Nissan and hustled over to climb in. The last thing he wanted was to have to walk home tonight.

*****

Callum Lange was up in a Douglas fir tree the next morning when Suleka pulled in, buckling a trail camera to the trunk. He'd thought about this a lot during the night, when he'd found himself wide awake, staring up at the glow from the moon spilling in through the skylight in the pinnacle of his yurt. He'd bought this trail camera to watch for wildlife on his property but there was no reason he couldn't use it for security too. What was it Suleka had said? He had to think like a pirate to catch a pirate.

The Nissan chugged down the driveway and Lange tucked his head in close to the camera. Sure enough, he heard the clicking sound of photos being taken as the Nissan pulled into view and parked in front of his yurt. This was definitely the right place for it.

Suleka climbed out of the truck and began walking towards his tree. "You need me to drive you around this morning?"

"If you would."

She looked up at him, one eye closed against the morning sun. "That nice Prius of yours will turn into rodent habitat if you don't drive it every once in a while."

"I drive it!"

"Not very often."

"I don't prefer to drive, you know that, not after the stress of driving in New York City."

"I don't prefer to drive either but I do it."

He creased his brow at her. "So what are you saying? You *don't* want to drive me around this morning?"

"No, I'm saying that's a nice Prius you've got sitting outside the Ranger Station at Rockport State Park. Nicer than my old pick-up."

"You want to drive my Prius instead of your truck?"

She thought for a second. "Probably not. Does it have one of those new-fangled start buttons?"

"Uh-huh."

"Then definitely not."

"So why did you....?" Lange stopped himself, knowing that trying to make sense out of the conversation they'd just had was futile. He changed track. "How did you see me without even looking?"

"You should know me by now," she replied, flicking her eyes towards the view over the valley. "I see everything."

He huffed and started to climb down the tree. He did know her and he had to admit she was very observant. Others were rarely so observant. Although, he thought, as he looked over his shoulder and stretched his right leg out to touch his toes on the ground, someone had spotted his firewood pile and knew when he was gone, so he definitely shouldn't get complacent. That's how they'd managed to steal from him in the first place. His left foot dropped down to meet the right and he dipped forward to brush off his sweatpants.

"What were you doing up there?" Suleka asked, looking up in the tree again. "Oh, I see it now. Very clever. Is that for your firewood thief or the deer?"

"Both, if I'm lucky." He straightened up and stepped away. His chest puffed out as he filled his lungs with morning, mountain air. It was perfectly chill, like good white wine, and smelled like fresh oxygen and icy dew and boundless amounts of chlorophyll. Not that any of those things necessarily had an aroma but that's what Lange liked most; the absence of smells. Garbage smells, subway smells, exhaust smells, sewer smells, all the things that permeated the streets of NYC.

"We got a good solid frost last night," mentioned Suleka, her eyes on the patches of white twinkling across the ground in the morning sunlight.

Lange felt newly invigorated. "What time is it?" he asked, striding towards the yurt.

Suleka trotted along beside him. "Ten till eight."

"That's kind of early for you, isn't it?"

"Tell me about it," she groaned. Then justified her early arrival with, "Deller sent me. Got any coffee made?"

"Sitting on the woodstove," nodded Lange.

"Good. I'll fill you in over a cup."

They climbed up the steps and Lange motioned Suleka to go in as he slipped off his dark brown rubber sandals. He stepped over the threshold and immediately his cold, bare feet appreciated the radiant floor heat. He lingered a moment, flexing his toes, before crossing to his sleeping area. "Help yourself," he said, pointing at the ceramic drip coffee pot sitting on the woodstove. "I'm going to change my pants, so don't look."

"Wouldn't dream of it," Suleka shot back, looking down at the coffee pot. She lifted it off the woodstove and turned her back on Lange to carry it over to the kitchen area. "Want me to pour you a cup too?" she asked as she set the pot down on the counter next to the sink.

"Thanks, yes," Lange replied. He pulled off his sweatpants, deposited them at the foot of his bed and climbed into his jeans.

Suleka lifted two mugs made by the local potter out of the dish drainer and set them next to the coffee pot. She took the ceramic filter off the top of the pot and filled each mug with dark, aromatic coffee. "Got any milk?" she asked, opening the door to the refrigerator.

Lange was sitting on the bed, pulling on some wool socks. "Don't think so," he answered.

Suleka looked for the quart she'd bought last time she'd gone shopping for Lange but didn't see it. "Boy, you get through milk fast," she remarked, closing the fridge. She picked up both mugs of coffee and, without turning around, called out, "You decent?"

"Yep," he replied.

He stood up and they crossed the yurt towards each other, meeting at his desk in the center. "How's the writing going?" she asked, handing him his coffee.

"Better." He lifted the mug to his lips and let the strong, slightly bitter scent tease his palette before taking a gulp. The warmth flowed through his chest and hit the pit of his stomach. "Did you find out about the thefts?"

"I did. I got names and places and I can point out most of them as we head over to Mary Lynn McCracken's house this morning."

Lange gave her a piercing look. "Why are we going there?"

"Because she was the last person that Margi spoke to on Friday night. *And* she was the one that called Margi on Saturday morning."

"The missed call."

"Exactly."

"So she *didn't* just wait for Margi to call her."

"That's what Deller wants you to go find out."

"Is she even home?"

"Who, Mary Lynn?"

Lange nodded.

Suleka was sipping her coffee and made a 'darned if I know' face over the rim of the mug at him. "Deller said the retreat ended at breakfast today so she figured Mary Lynn's either home or on her way home. And if she's not home she said you can do some scouting with the SAR dogs around the Breckenridge place. They got there at first light."

Lange was shaking his head no as he gulped down some more coffee. "I want to talk to the girlfriend."

"She works down valley....."

"Not before noon. I already checked with Collins." He marched over to the kitchen and set his empty coffee cup on the counter. "You ready?"

Suleka moved her mug around in the air, as if she were looking for a place to set it but was not quite ready to let go of it.

"Bring that with you," ordered Lange. He had the door open already to leave.

"Do you even know where she lives?" she called out after him.

"Marblemount," he called back, slipping his feet into his Redwings outside the door.

Suleka gulped down the last of her coffee and set the mug down on his desk just to annoy him. She hoped he'd know more than just "Marblemount" by the time they got up there.

*****

The drive up to Marblemount was much more pleasant than the interview with Breckenridge's girlfriend, Shelby. The fall colors on the trees rising up the ridges alongside the highway made brushstrokes of warm orange and soft gold through the landscape of evergreens. The field of blueberry bushes just before the farm stand was such a burnished copper-crimson that Lange made Suleka pull over so he could take a photo with his phone. But Shelby, a petite, full-bodied brunette whose hair stood out from her head like she'd had an electric shock, took the mellow right out of Lange's mind with her surly tongue and abrasive manner. Pointing her finger at his chest she made it clear that she had nothing to do with Margi Breckenridge, other than sleeping with her husband, and that she didn't intend to waste her time answering any of his questions, especially since they were probably the same questions that the Sheriff's Deputy had asked her last night. And she knew her rights!

Lange sighed inwardly. He probably had enough of an impression of this snippy young woman to leave it at that but he felt compelled to push a little further. "Aren't you concerned for Sam Breckenridge that his wife is missing?" he asked.

"No," she retorted. "He was gonna leave her for me anyway."

"Are you sure about that?"

She put one hand on her hip and flashed her large, dark eyes at him, trying to appear alluring, Lange guessed. "Wouldn't you?" she said.

He held back the retort that came to mind and tried one last time to get the facts. "And you were in Eastern Washington Saturday morning?" he said.

"I told you, ask that other Deputy. I have to get ready for work."

Once Lange and Suleka were safely inside the Nissan again she made her assessment. "If I were Sam, I'd stick with Margi. She's much nicer than that little vixen."

"Maybe he'd already come to that conclusion," Lange mused.

Suleka stared at him, intrigued, as she turned the key in the ignition. "And if she knew that's what he was thinking...." she added.

They let the idea hover as the Nissan crossed the green metal bridge over the Cascade River and started down the Rockport-Cascade Road, Lange with his eyes on the sunlight, dancing on the surface of the water, and Suleka hunched over the steering wheel, her head tilted in contemplation. Having turned it over in his mind every which way the ex-detective from NYC finally sighed. "But she was away all weekend."

"What if," Suleka theorized, "Shelby planned a meeting with Margi for when she got back?"

Lange faced her. "To what purpose?"

"To talk about Sam."

"But then why would Margi go?"

"What if it was Margi that wanted the meeting?"

Lange caught on immediately. "Because Sam *was* talking about leaving her..."

"And she wanted to talk Shelby into backing off. Or at least leaving some room for her in the picture."

"So Shelby agrees as long as it can be someplace in Marblemount...."

"Where she knows Margi goes wildcrafting...."

"At a time when she knows Sam won't be home."

Suleka's enthusiasm for the idea rose. "I mean, there's nothing to say that she's been missing since Saturday morning."

Lange opened his mouth to agree but then his enthusiasm deflated. "Except the dog food."

"What?"

He stared out the passenger window at the river again. If the bowl hadn't been so full he could believe Margi had left as late as

Sunday afternoon.

"What about the dog food?" Suleka insisted.

But Margi must have been planning to be away to leave so much food out for the dog. No, there was no way she'd only been gone since Sunday afternoon.

Suleka hit the steering wheel with the heel of her hand and snapped, "Don't you know how frustrating it is when you leave me out of the discussion?!"

"What's that?" said Lange, completely unaware of her torture.

She pushed her lips up to her nose indignantly; he could be so dense. "Nothing," she mumbled.

Lange sat forward as Suleka swung to the left, pulling into a short gravel driveway with a brown, rambler style house at the end of it. A silver Taurus with a yellow bumper sticker that said Grandma's Taxi was parked in front of the house and a woman, leaning into the trunk, stood upright as they arrived and gave them an unwelcoming glare; a stout, middle-aged woman with teased dark hair and red lipstick to match her red and black checked jacket. "Is that Mary Lynn?'

"Uh-huh," said Suleka.

"Has she lived upriver long?"

"A few years I think. Why?"

"I don't know. She looks more suburban than upriver."

Suleka laughed. "Well that's Mary Lynn for you."

She switched off the engine and they moved at the same time to get out of the Nissan. Mary Lynn marched towards them, her black pants flapping against her short heels. "What do you..." She stopped as the stern in her face suddenly changed to delight. "Oh hi, Suleka!"

"Hi, Mary Lynn."

"I didn't know you were coming over today."

"Well it wasn't planned." Suleka held her right hand out, palm up, preparing to introduce Lange, but Mary Lynn continued on as if he weren't there.

"Oh I wish you could have come to the Women's Retreat up at Baker Lake. You would have really loved it."

"Is that right?"

"Everyone was so friendly and it was peaceful and relaxing. Plus the food was amazing. They made primarily vegetarian dishes, all organic of course, and...."

"I'm sorry to interrupt," stated Lange, not feeling sorry at all but doing his best to sound sorry. "But we're under a time constraint here."

"It's about Margi Breckenridge," Suleka added. "You know she's missing?"

Mary Lynn's forehead creased. "Yes, I heard."

Lange reached his hand out to meet hers. "I'm Callum Lange," he said, "and I'd like to ask you a few questions."

Her mouth made a little O of surprise and then her face lit up like a kid's on a merry-go-round. "*You're* Callum Lange!" she gushed. "I've heard so much about you. I keep telling Suleka every time I see her, which is not that often because..."

Lange retrieved his hand from her grasp and interrupted again. "I believe you were the last person to speak to Margi Breckenridge before she went missing."

"Was I?"

"You spoke to her Friday night."

"I did," agreed Mary Lynn, "We needed to confab about whether she was coming to the Retreat or not and how I'd find out what she decided but I didn't know that made me the last person to speak to her. How spooky." She wrapped her open jacket across her chest in folded arms as if the thought made her want to hunker down against the cold.

"You told Deputy Collins that you waited for Margi's call to know whether you should stop by and pick her up for the retreat. When she didn't call, you just headed up to Baker Lake without her?"

"That's right."

"Except you didn't."

Lange thought he saw a fissure of fear cross her face but it was gone so quickly he couldn't be sure. "What's that?" she said.

"You didn't *just* wait for her call and then leave when you didn't get one. You called her on Saturday morning."

Mary Lynn McCracken frowned like she didn't understand.

"There was a missed call from you on Margi's phone," Suleka explained.

Lange bit down on the urge to scold Suleka. She should have waited for Mary Lynn to give it up without prompting. Maybe some training was in order.

But Mary Lynn seemed grateful for the reminder. "That's right! I *did* call Margi. I guess I really wanted her to come with me and, well, you know how bad cell phone reception can be up here." She was looking at Suleka whose phone chirruped in her pocket at that very moment as if to disprove the point. Suleka looked surprised, then walked away to answer the call, coming to a stop at the open trunk end of Mary Lynn's car. "Well it is," Mary Lynn argued to Lange. "People are always leaving me voicemails that I don't get until I'm closer to the cell tower in Concrete so I thought maybe I should check. But Margi didn't pick up." Her face became glum. "I wish she had come with me. We wouldn't be here now if she'd come."

Lange thought for a moment, watching the frost making big, silvery drips on the bottoms of the pendulous cedar tree branches as it melted in the morning sunshine. "If you were worried about cell phone reception," he said finally, bringing his focus back to Mary Lynn, "why didn't you just stop by on Saturday morning to see if Margi wanted to go?"

"I thought about it." She darted a look at Suleka, who was ending her phone conversation. "But I can be kind of pushy and I didn't want to *make* her come."

Lange nodded, as if he understood. Suleka walked back towards them and he could tell by the way she was looking at him that she had something important to confer. He just had one more question for Mary Lynn. "And you knew Margi was missing how?"

"I stopped at the grocery store on my way home and overheard someone talking about it."

"Albert's was open that early?" Suleka sounded surprised. She pulled her pocket watch out to check the time.

"I meant the gas station by the Baker Lake Highway," Mary Lynn put in quickly. "I stopped there to pick up a few groceries and the Concrete Herald because I knew it was too early for Albert's."

But Lange had seen the flush on her cheekbones, had heard the backpedalling in her voice, and he knew they'd just caught her in a lie. What baffled him was why would she lie about where she heard the news?

*****

"What time does Albert's open?" Lange rapped out as soon as they cleared McCracken's driveway.

"Nine."

"And what time is it now?"

"Nine-ten." Suleka turned left on the Rockport-Cascade Road, heading for Highway 530.

"We'd better get a move on. That took a lot longer than I thought it would. Who was on the phone?"

"Charlotte. She owns the Inn on the South Skagit, just east of Concrete. Well, she and her girls own it. Anyway, she told me that one of her guests had a hand-painted gourd with wolves on it and she wondered if it was one of the ones Margi painted."

"Was it?" The news had Lange on the edge of his seat, looking directly at Suleka.

"Well she didn't know. That's why she called us, so we'd come look at it."

"It's still there."

"I guess. Yes. Well I'm not sure but..."

"How did she know about Margi's wildlife gourds?"

"I told her." Suleka thought about this. "No, maybe I didn't tell *her* exactly but I'm pretty sure I told Kathy who either told Charlotte or Liz. And Liz would have told Charlotte."

"I hope you're not gossiping about our cases."

"I wouldn't call it gossiping...."

"But you tell locals information pertinent to the investigation?" Lange could feel himself getting more and more irate. They passed the Breckenridge place on the left, Search and Rescue vehicles plugging the driveway, and continued on, without getting distracted, to Highway 530.

Suleka was unapologetic. "If I think they need to know it, then yes, sure I do."

"They don't need to know anything," Lange voiced emphatically. "Only *I* need to know it until the case is solved."

"Then why did you send me off to find out who'd been burglarized?" Suleka reasoned. "I can't get that information without talking to people and talking means answering their questions so they can determine if they want to help or not."

"Why wouldn't they want to help?"

"The Upper Valley is a small community, Cal. Nobody's going to tell you anything they don't want you to know. Anyway, I don't know what you're getting so worked up about. My telling Liz or Charlotte....or maybe it was Nancy, I don't remember, but my telling somebody about Margi's artwork led to Charlotte calling us."

"Which may not be of *any* help!" Lange stressed.

"That's true. But what if it is one of Margi's gourds? Whoever has it must have bought it from Margi, which means Margi took those gourds somewhere to sell. Which is how come we couldn't find them on her property. And presumably she took them somewhere on Saturday morning, without telling anyone where she was going, and maybe she's still there."

"Where?!"

"Wherever she sold the gourd!" Suleka hesitated, as if waiting for him to comment but when he didn't she went on with her theorizing. "Or maybe she made enough money to buy a bus ticket to Vegas and she's on her way to have some fun."

"Did she ever talk about going to Vegas?"

"No, I don't mean *Vegas* exactly. I mean…well she could have gone to…." She had her right hand up in the air and Lange waited for her to name the place that would appeal to Margi. But nothing came. Instead she grabbed the steering wheel again and snapped, "Well, you know what I mean."

"No, I don't - because if Margi ran off to kick up her heels she would have taken Coco with her."

"Well that's just one theory. I'm not saying it actually happened. I'm just saying it's a good job I mentioned these gourds in the phone tree because it made Charlotte call us when she saw one."

"And I'm saying you should keep your mouth shut when we're working on a case."

"Hah!"

"Hah?"

"You'll be saying that out of the other side of your mouth when you see where this gourd leads us!"

Lange chomped down on his irritation and thought about her statement as they crossed the narrow bridge over the Skagit River. Suleka's idea might have some validity but still she needed to know when to hold her tongue. Or maybe just when to stop acting like a friend to the locals he was questioning and start acting more like a detective's assistant. He snorted as they pulled up to the intersection with Hwy 20; what in the world was he thinking?! He wasn't a detective out here on Sauk Mountain and Suleka had never agreed to be any kind of detective's assistant. A little shopping and the occasional cleaning of his yurt, that's what she'd agreed to when they'd met. It was just bad luck that she'd ended up driving him to a couple of crime scenes. Bad luck for her, that is, because he'd found her pretty helpful. Detective Deller, the only real detective in this whole set-up, must have thought so too because Suleka was the one she called when she needed Lange's help.

The Nissan turned left onto the highway. Deller hadn't called him with the lab results yet, and it was what? – he slipped his cell phone out of his jacket pocket and looked – 9:16 am. He focused on Suleka again, curious. "Did Deller tell you whether those items we found at the Breckenridge place revealed anything significant?" They came around a bend in the road and he saw the big trees of Rockport State Park. Suleka said nothing. "Did she?" Lange prodded. But again she was silent. Two small deer were browsing under the trees at the edge of the highway, but Lange couldn't see them through the cloud of hostility fogging up the inside of the truck. "Oh what? Now you're not talking to me?' he groused.

Suleka pounced. "No, I'm keeping my mouth shut. Just like you said,"

"I didn't mean when talking to me!"

"Well how am I supposed to know the difference?" The words were innocent enough but Lange saw sarcasm in the curl of her lip. "Best I keep my mouth shut at all times."

They were at the gates to the State park and Lange glanced right, to check on his Prius parked at the Ranger's house, when he was distracted by the sight of some people coming out of the end of Sauk Mountain Road. Three people on foot, one markedly smaller than the other two, pulling a Red Rider Wagon full of........ "Firewood!" he yelled, pointing ahead at the boys now walking west on Hwy 20. "That's my firewood!!"

"What do you want me to...?"

"Pull over! Pull over!!"

Suleka stomped on the brakes and jerked the truck over to the hard shoulder. Lange tumbled out before the Nissan came to a complete stop. "Freeze!" he yelled and three heads spun in his direction. That's when he realized he knew these kids. Liked them even. And had helped them more than once. His surprise that they were stealing from him must have hit at the same moment as their surprise that he'd caught them because they suddenly dumped the red wagon and hightailed it away from him. Lange immediately gave chase; they might be young and fast but he was practiced and he wasn't going to let them escape without an explanation. The world around him narrowed to the sound of his breath, huffing in and out of his nose, and the beat of his feet on the asphalt pulsing in his ears.

And then an explosion – BAM! – and his left shoulder kicked back so violently his feet came out from under him and slammed him to the ground. A searing pain burned through his collarbone and he groaned, snatching at it with his right hand to try to make it stop. Somewhere through the thick fog inside his head he heard a voice, frantic, beside him. "Cal, are you okay? Are you okay?"

"Go! Go!" Lange whispered, waving down the street with his right hand. That's when he saw the blood. He looked down to find a dark stain creeping across his shirt from the fire in his chest. He flopped back, writhing in agony.

"Are you okay?" the voice said again.

"I told you to go," Lange insisted.

"I'm not chasing after those boys! I know exactly who they are and where they live, I don't need to give myself a stroke trying to catch them."

The fog began to lift at the matter-of-factness in the voice and Lange opened his eyes to see Suleka, kindly Suleka, leaning over him. Suleka, not Jimmy Vonortas.

"Are you okay?" she asked again.

"I don't know," he said, confused. "Am I?"

"You fell down but I don't know that you're hurt." Her eyes

were searching up and down his body and he suddenly felt exposed and embarrassed. He knew he was on the ground for no reason other than memory. Something had thrown him back to the streets of New York.

"I heard an explosion," he offered sheepishly, sitting up and brushing himself off.

"A car backfired..."

"That must have been it." He stood up and looked down the highway. The boys were gone. But he also knew where they lived and he felt foolish for running after them. Even more foolish for thinking he'd been shot.

"Why did you fall down?" Suleka asked, as they walked back towards the Nissan.

"I just," Lange started, then realized he'd have to listen to a million questions and maybe he wasn't ready for that. Not yet. Not without a whiskey in his hand. "I tripped," he said.

Suleka looked at him. She knew he was lying but she also sensed this wasn't the time to push it. "Well get in," she said. "Charlotte has other things to do than wait on us."

"Can we stop at the boys' house first?"

"We'd better. Because I have some questions for them!"

*****

They rode down the hill and turned left, preparing to drop down to the singlewide mobile home where the boys lived. But there was no need. All three boys had stopped running and were scuffing their awkward-sized feet in an unhurried, teenage way along the gravel road, heads down, shaggy hair flopping down into their eyes. They were brothers, Zach, Casey and Seth, the two oldest blond and fair skinned, and Seth, the youngest, stockier and darker. Different dads. Lange didn't know for sure but guessed Seth was ten or eleven and the other boys closer to fifteen. He had interacted a number of times with all three of them and never would have guessed they'd steal from him. He rolled down his window and yelled, "Hey I want my firewood back!"

This time the boys didn't bother to act surprised. "You can have it," said Zach.

"We never even wanted to steal it," piped in Seth, his voice high with childish indignation. "And it wasn't us that took your milk!"

"What milk?" Lange was confused.

"And what do you mean, you never wanted to steal it?!" Suleka was caustic.

They all three spoke at the same time.

"We were gonna pay for it...."

"You weren't home..."

"We didn't know how much..."

"What milk?!" insisted Lange.

Casey took control of the explanation. "We came to buy firewood, like, three days ago, but you weren't there so we figured we'd walked all that way, may as well take a coupla armloads and make it right with you next time."

His brothers joined in. "But then you weren't there again yesterday."

"And it was cold."

"So we took some more."

"But we have money."

"Or we'll work."

"Whatever you want," Casey ended.

"Why didn't your mother just drive you up to buy wood?" Suleka interjected and the boys looked at each other and down at the ground so quickly that their embarrassment could have been missed. But it wasn't.

"What milk?!" Lange asked for a third time.

"The milk in your fridge," Seth said like this should have been obvious.

"You went into my yurt?!"

"No! But we've seen that guy go in twice now and both times leave with a quart of milk."

Suleka puckered her lips in irony. "No wonder you're always out."

"Which guy?" Lange wanted to know.

"The one with the long hair that's always sneaking through the woods."

"You've seen him?"

"Sometimes. But he moves fast."

"Does your mother know you're roaming the woods when you're s'posed to be in school?" Suleka admonished and again the brothers became sheepish. She wasn't about to ignore it a second time. "What's going on?" she demanded. "Where's your mother?"

Hurried glances from underneath fallen fringes and shuffling of feet indicated they really didn't want to say but Lange knew they would if he could just wait. He shot Suleka the full force of his clear blue eyes to hold her tongue. She took the hint. A ten count later, Casey reluctantly admitted, "She took off on a drug binge with her new boyfriend."

Lange absorbed this then asked, "Is that why I've been seeing you walking the highway up to Rockport so much lately?"

They nodded. "To get groceries."

Suleka's hackles went up immediately. "She left you alone in the house with no groceries?!"

"And no wood," added Lange.

The brothers glance at each other then back at Lange. "We don't want anyone to know."

"Else they'll split us up. Put us into care."

Lange checked with Suleka, who pulled one side of her mouth back into her cheek like she didn't know. The brothers had only been living in the Upper Valley a few years, when mom had moved in with her previous boyfriend, but they'd obviously adjusted to life in the woods. Lange could understand their reluctance to move again, especially if it meant being separated. "Alright," he declared. "Come up to my place when Suleka is there with the Nissan and you can load it up with wood."

"And it's okay for us to work it off?" Casey asked.

"Sure." Lange didn't care whether they paid for the wood or not but he knew they'd feel more comfortable giving him some hours. Then a thought occurred to him. "How come you ran if you were planning to pay me?"

More glances and shuffling and Lange realized they didn't have a clue. They'd run from instinct rather than guilt. He let it go. "Can you show me where this milk thief wanders?"

"Okay," they agreed.

"It'll have to be later though."

"After school."

"You're not *in* school," Suleka reminded them.

"Two hour late start," Seth shot back.

"Good. *Good!*" Lange emphasized, leaning forward in his seat. "Don't want to give Child Protective cause to come looking for you."

"Yeah," agreed Zach. "Plus it's warm at school."

"School bus!" Seth snapped at his brothers, eyes bulging, fleshy cheeks quivering with urgency. They glanced up at the highway as their feet began moving away.

"Gotta go," Casey said over his shoulder to Lange.

Suleka let the Nissan drift along the road beside them. "We'll pick you up from school at 2:30," she said through the open window. The sound of a growling diesel engine became louder and she glimpsed school bus yellow in her rear view mirror.

"Okay," agreed the brothers, stopping in the middle of a wide spot in the road.

Suleka lifted herself up in the driver's seat and craned her neck around to keep talking to them as the Nissan coasted by. "I'll take you grocery shopping later too if you want." They turned away and she heard the accordion expulsion of air as the school bus stopped in the middle of the road. She put her foot down on the gas, moving the Nissan forward towards Highway 20 and the Inn. "One mystery solved," she announced, relieved. Lange sucked softly on the plate in his mouth. The road narrowed as the Skagit River came in on their left. They both jumped as a bald eagle leapt off an overhanging hemlock tree branch directly in front of them. Its large, brown body dipped scarily close to the Nissan before the action of its wings, flapping hard and tight, propelled the magnificent, white-headed bird upwards. "That was close," Suleka grimaced, the white tail feathers zig-zagging through a dense patch of trees to their right before disappearing.

Still Lange said nothing. He was watching the bird but thinking about the brothers wandering onto his property when he wasn't there. Maybe he should talk to them about that. Not that he necessarily wanted to deny them access to his place because having them around periodically was a way to keep an eye on things when he wasn't home. But he'd prefer to be informed immediately if they saw something unusual. Like the guy stealing his milk; who knew how many quarts he'd furnished for this fellow? If they'd left him a note saying what they'd seen, he would have hung his trail camera sooner.

He yawned, arching his chest towards the sun pouring through the windshield now that they were on Highway 20, heading for Concrete. "You want to tell me about the shooting?" demanded Suleka and his moment in the sun was over. "What shooting?" he queried, cautious.

"The one that caused you to do a header when you heard that car backfire."

He felt himself slump; she'd figured it out. "It was nothing."

"Didn't look like nothing the way you were squirming around with your face all scrunched up."

They were crossing the Baker River and Lange looked past Suleka to where the Baker met the Skagit; usually they were two bodies of limestone fed green water but today, the Skagit was a torrent of glacial melt chocolate milk. "We were chasing a suspect," Lange began, letting his two worlds come together. "In the Bronx. I could hear my partner gaining on me from behind, when suddenly the suspect flipped around and shot at us. Next thing I knew I was on the ground, with my shoulder on fire with pain. Like someone had drilled a red hot poker into my collarbone and left it there."

Suleka glanced over at him. His fingers had crept towards a spot on his left collarbone. "You weren't wearing a vest?"

Lange shrugged. "We were detectives. We weren't expecting a shoot out."

"Did you catch the guy?"

Lange nodded. "My partner, Jimmy, chased him around a corner and caught him scrambling up a metal fence. He screamed at him to freeze but the guy kept climbing so Jimmy shot. When that didn't slow him down, Jimmy shot again. But the guy made it over the top of the fence and kept on running. About 30 paces later he crumpled into a heap. Dead." He rubbed the scar through his fleece jacket. "We think it was adrenaline that kept him going."

Suleka slowed, to let a logging truck go past her, then turned to cross the Skagit over the Dalles Bridge. "I can't imagine," she sighed.

"You're better off not," Lange told her. He sat forward, leaving New York City behind him, and looked past Suleka at middle Finney Ridge. Finney Creek came down from the mountains towards the Skagit and then turned left, to run parallel to the river for a good ten miles, then it dropped in south of the Dalles Bridge. He remembered when he was a boy, out visiting his uncle Glen for the summer, how they would stand at the side of Finney Creek, watching sunlight dapple the water braiding in and out around a myriad of tiny islands. His uncle would explain that the flatness of the creek meant the water flowed evenly, making it perfect for fishing. Lots of spawning grounds and not too many water pools. They'd tie on some lures and catch their limit of long, beautiful Cutthroat trout.

Lange felt a sad sweetness settle on him, like he'd said goodbye to a loved one. Finney Ridge was made almost entirely of sediment and glacial debris and intensive logging had caused sloughing and sliding, silting up the creek water and putting an end to the fishing. He clucked at the roof of his mouth.

"What?" Suleka asked, as they headed down the South Skagit, towards The Inn.

"This gourd better be worth the trip," was all he said back.

*****

Fortunately it was. A handsome older woman with a halo of white hair and peaches and cream complexion was standing at the door to the Inn when they pulled up. "That's Charlotte," said Suleka as she switched off the engine.

"She was waiting for us?"

"No. She probably saw us coming up the driveway and recognizes that you're on a timeline."

"I like her already," Lange declared, throwing open his door. His nostrils caught the slightly acrid aroma of manure and newly turned earth. "Good morning," he called out over the welcome barks from two large dogs.

"You made it," Charlotte replied and her face lit up in a coquettish smile. Lange returned the smile and let the barking dominate while he admired the impressive collection of classic tractors and gently rusted tillers ornamenting the top of the driveway. He walked around the Nissan taking in the acres of verdant pasture that fed the herd of prize Maine-Anjou cattle and then his eyes lifted and his breath caught at the sight of Mount Baker, sitting like a pinnacle of shiny white meringue in the sky opposite. Nice view, he thought.

"You coming?" asked Suleka from the doorway.

"Mmm hmm," he murmured. He pulled himself away and strode up a ramp to follow Suleka into the Inn. The painted gourd was sitting on a short length of counter just inside the door with Charlotte standing just beyond it, her hands folded tidily in front of her like a teacher waiting for an answer.

Suleka flattened herself against a bookcase in the narrow reception area, giving Lange room to bend forward and examine the gourd. Three wolves stared out at him, their yellow eyes piercing through his soul to the wilderness beyond, and he felt a curious inclination to run his hand over the charcoal tips of their sepia toned coats to see if they were as soft as they looked. He straightened up, lifted the gourd and turned it over and around, looking for a signature. But there wasn't one. He gently placed it back on the counter, slipped his phone out of his pocket and took a photograph, just in case. But it definitely looked like Margi's work to him. He heard a whisper, like a breeze in the air, or a sigh, and glanced around. Charlotte was watching him, gauging his response to the gourd with her soft blue eyes, and he felt like he was in the presence of Miss Marple and should watch his Ps and Qs. "This belongs to one of your guests?" he asked, slipping his phone back in his pocket.

Charlotte nodded. "She brought it down to show us at breakfast this morning, she was so proud of it. As soon as I saw it I remembered what Suleka had told Emily..."

"It was *Emily*," acknowledged Suleka.

"And I asked the woman if I could hold on to it for a while, to show a friend. I didn't say who or why of course."

Lange looked across at Suleka; someone knew how to hold their tongue.

"My guest agreed even though this gourd was expensive. She trusts me," Charlotte finished with an honest nod and a blink.

Lange wanted to squeeze her, he was so delighted she'd acted this quickly, but he managed to refrain. "Did your guest say where she purchased the gourd?"

The innkeeper nodded again. "Up at the Women's Retreat." She hesitated. "Mary Lynn McCracken sold it to her."

"Mary *Lynn* did?!" wailed Suleka. Lange shot her a look. "What?" she said, "I never would have thought…"

He put a palm up in front of her. "We don't know the story yet."

"I suppose. But she never told us…"

Lange lifted his eyebrows and Suleka zipped it. He looked back at Charlotte. "Can you hold onto this gourd for the time being?"

"The woman's staying through tomorrow so until then, yes. But after that…" She furrowed her brow, worried.

"I hope we won't need it after that."

"And I hope you find Margi," said Charlotte, looking down at the gourd again. She leaned forward and cupped it pragmatically with her left hand. "She's so talented."

Lange heard the whisper again and felt a surge run though him, like a vein of certainty he was on the right track. "Let's go," he told Suleka and opened the door to leave.

"He's not very good at goodbyes," he heard her mutter to Charlotte.

"No need," said Charlotte. "I understand."

Lange was sure that she did. "Thank you!" he called out when he got to his side of the Nissan.

"You come back some time for tea now."

"Only if you promise to put something stronger than tea in it," he joked and heard a peal of laughter before he slid into his seat.

Suleka plopped down beside him, looking like she'd eaten something sour. "Back to Mary Lynn's?" she asked.

"As fast as you can."

She followed the command, starting up the truck and maneuvering it to go back down the driveway, while making it obvious that this was the last thing she wanted to do. "I just can't fathom how Mary Lynn could have been involved with Margi's disappearance!"

Before she could look at him, expecting a reply, Lange's phone rang. He recognized the number as Deller's. "Have you got the lab results?" he asked, in place of a greeting.

But Deller had her own thread she was following. "Did you notice whether Sam Breckenridge's girlfriend was wearing an engagement ring when you questioned her? Something with diamonds in it?"

"She was not," Lange replied without hesitation. He watched Mount Baker disappear as Suleka drove back towards the Dalles Bridge and Highway 20. She'd chosen the faster route despite her reluctance.

"You sound sure."

"I am. She kept waving her hands in my face and pointing and I noticed purple nail polish, tattoos on both wrists and a lot of metal ornamentation. No diamonds."

"Seriously?" said Deller. "That's his type?"

Lange decided not to touch that one. "What have you found?" he asked.

"A pawn shop receipt for a diamond ring. Breckenridge broke down when we questioned him about it and admitted that he bought the ring for his girlfriend a couple of weeks ago then changed his mind and decided to give it to Margi instead. But he can't tell us where the ring is."

"Maybe it's with Margi."

"He'd tell me that."

"He would if he knew."

"Oh. You're thinking she might have found the ring and took it with her wherever she went."

"That's one theory."

"Hmm." Deller chewed on this for a second. "But there's more."

"Tell me." The Nissan picked up speed as they exited the town limits of Concrete and Lange let his mind ski the surface of the Skagit rushing down valley while they rushed up.

"Search and Rescue dogs followed a trail from the house down to the creek, twice. There was blood where they stopped."

Lange groaned. "That doesn't sound good."

"Nope. We're getting it tested."

"What about the lab results on last night's findings?"

"Too soon. At least, it was before I left this morning to join the search. But I asked them to put a push on it so I'm hoping. Where are you?"

"On our way back to Mary Lynn McCracken's house." Lange filled Deller in on his morning; his interviews with Shelby and Mary Lynn, the phone call about one of Margi's wildlife gourds and his subsequent trip to the Inn to see it.

"You're sure it's her work?"

"Positive. But I took a photo just in case McCracken tries to argue the opposite with me."

"You don't want to stop and show the photo to Breckenridge, just in case."

"Don't need to. But I'll text you the photo if you're worried and you can show it to him."

"I'm not there anymore. I'm on my way down river already, for a debriefing with Search and Rescue. Then I hope the lab will have some news for me and after that, I think I might spring a surprise visit on Breckenridge's girlfriend at work."

"I told you I questioned her already."

"I know. But we found a threatening letter from her to Margi. 'You'd better agree to a divorce or else' kind-of-thing."

"Maybe she does have the ring and is hiding it till this settles."

"Maybe. I don't know why Sam wouldn't have told us that though."

"Fear," suggested Lange.

"Yeah," Deller said, long and slow like it was a possibility but not one she favored. "I don't get the impression he's savvy enough to be scared."

"Funny," said Lange. "I thought the same thing." They'd just crossed the Skagit River at Rockport and Lange was gazing through the woods to his right, watching the sun make patterns like filaments of spun sugar on the fall foliage, when his eyes caught a shadow. He did a double take and saw the distinct outline of a person, moving at a clip through the understory. "There he is!" he shouted.

"Who is?" asked Suleka.

"What's that?" came Deller.

"The man in the mud room!" said Lange.

"*Where*?" shouted Deller.

Suleka immediately took her foot off the gas. "You want me to pull over?"

Lange had swiveled around in his seat and was trying to keep his eye fixed on the moving shape, but they were too far past and the woods too brushy. "No," he said, turning back to face front and hanging up the phone without thinking about it. "Let get the MacCracken interview over with. See if we can't get her to confess to being somewhere other than where she *said* she was on Saturday morning."

*****

"Okay, so I did go over to Margi's house on Saturday," Mary Lynn McCracken admitted when Lange braced her with the fact that they'd discovered her sale of Margi's gourd. "But it's not what you're thinking which is why I didn't tell you the first time you asked."

She and Sam Breckenridge must have gone to the same class on police thinking, Lange said to himself. They'd found Mary Lynn in her kitchen, piping orange frosting onto homemade pumpkin shaped cookies and Lange was having trouble keeping his eyes off what she was doing and on her face. Clever ploy, he thought, and touched her wrist to get her attention. "Tell us now," he said.

She stopped, obviously considering his request, then laid down her icing bag and began. "Margi called me Friday night, as you know, and told me that she *wanted* to go to the Women's Retreat but she wasn't sure she was up to it. She was depressed. I asked her what was up and she became vague so I knew she must be really depressed because Margi always tells me *everything!*" She overemphasized the word, as if sometimes "everything" was more than she wanted to hear. "It was something about a letter. That much I found out, but she didn't want to discuss it." Mary Lynn cut her eyes over to Suleka. "Of course, I knew about that tramp Shelby....."

"Everybody does."

"...and I suspected it had something to do with her but I didn't want to pry so I left it. And I told Margi to sleep on it and call me in the morning. I really thought she might change her mind about going to the Women's Retreat. That's when she told me she'd been planning to take her new wildlife gourds up there, to see what people thought."

Mary Lynn gazed off, preoccupied. When she pulled herself back she picked up a small tube of white frosting and began moving it confidently, ably, from one cookie to the next, adding touches to the orange. Her kitchen was warm and sweet smelling and Lange had to force himself to keep his eyes away from the repetitive motion of her hands. "Anyway," she went on, "Margi *didn't* call me on Saturday morning, as you know, and I decided to drive over to her house, just to check. One last try to see if I couldn't take her out of herself. I knocked on the door, opened it, called out, *"Margi,"* but no answer. So I went in and...." She stopped decorating and waved her hands around in the air, apologetic, embarrassed. "...well, her kitchen table's right there. I couldn't help but see the note."

"What note?" asked Lange.

"The one she left for Sam." Her eyes narrowed, waiting for a response. "He didn't tell you about the note?"

Lange shook his head no. He looked at Suleka; her mouth had dropped open. Mary Lynn turned to her, a plea in her voice. "I would never usually have read it, of course, but I was *worried* about her. Especially since I could see the word 'depressed' staring out at me from its sad little placement on the table. What if she'd done something to herself?" Suleka nodded, like she agreed. "I tried calling her before I picked up the note, thinking I could talk to her instead of reading her personal business, but when she didn't answer I realized that the phone I could hear ringing was hers, in her purse on the windowsill next to me." She glared at Lange, as if daring him to challenge her. "So I read it. It said she was depressed and lonely and hurt and that she was going away to think about things and he shouldn't try to find her." She ended with her hands in the air, as if that's all she knew, then went back to decorating her cookies. "I'm surprised Sam didn't show it to you."

"And I'm surprised you didn't tell us you knew Margi was missing before we did," Lange shot back.

She kept squeezing little blobs of white on the cookies. "Well I didn't know she was *missing* exactly. Just that she needed a moment away from Sam. There's a big difference between that and her going missing, don't you think?"

There was no way Lange was going to tell her what he thought. "What did you do with the note?"

"I put it back on the kitchen table, exactly where I found it. Except," she straightened up again, remembering, "it was leaning on a box of the gourds she'd told me about, and I decided to take those to the Women's Retreat for her, to see if I couldn't sell them." She laughed a slight, nervous expulsion of emotion. "I was thinking she might need the money if she was moving out on Sam, plus it would be a nice surprise for her if they sold. I leaned the note up against a coffee cup instead." She shrugged. "Maybe it fell down and Sam didn't see it."

An expert explanation for everything, Lange realized. As expert as the white frosting features she was putting on the cookies to make them look like carved pumpkins. "How many of Margi's gourds did you sell?" he asked.

Mary Lynn stood up and smiled a big, proud smile. "All of them! I made over four thousand dollars for Margi and I have it stashed away safely for when she comes back."

"Wow," said Suleka. "That's impressive. Did you sell any of yours too?"

Lange followed Suleka's eyes over to a round, basket weave tray on a counter next to the fridge. It was full of gourds with what looked like animal scenes painted on them. Oversimplified animal scenes from what he could tell at a distance. Not nearly the quality of Margi's work.

"Oh no," shuddered Mary Lynn, as though the question were distasteful. "I didn't take mine up there. It wasn't a sales event."

"Really?" The surprise in Suleka's voice made Lange look at her; something was up. "But you took Margi's," she said.

"Well that felt more like fundraising than selling. It was in keeping with the spirit of the retreat."

Mary Lynn ended looking self-satisfied, graced them both with a small smile and then screwed the top back on the tube of frosting. "If there's nothing else," she said and waved a hand over the cookies, "I need to get these finished so I can take them to my granddaughter's birthday party this afternoon."

Lange smiled disarmingly at Mary Lynn. "They look good," he said. "Where's the party?"

"Why?" she laughed, and dipped her head as if flirting with him. "Are you thinking of turning up to get your share?"

He patted his belly, still smiling. "No, I think I'll leave the kids to do the growing, not me. I was just hoping you'd be somewhere where you can get cell phone reception in case I need to follow up on our conversation."

She flapped her hand in the air at him. "Oh I get cell service pretty much anywhere."

"Just not here," Lange contended, and for the second time saw a crack in her composure.

"That's what you told us last time," Suleka put in.

"*Sometimes* not here, is what I think I said," Mary Lynn clarified, with a pedantic smile. "But anywhere west of here I'm good, and the party's in Birdsview, so...." She picked up the bag of orange frosting again.

"Can we get the address?" Lange asked, like it was no big deal.

"Birdsview is west of Concrete, detective."

"You can call me Cal," he replied, turning on the charm. She visibly softened so he went for the clincher. "Time is crucial in a missing person case and the information you've given me has been very helpful. I want to be sure I can catch you if I need to before the day's over."

"Well of course, in that case." She put down her frosting and tap tapped across the kitchen in her heels. "Let me just get some paper."

As soon as she was out of sight down a hallway, Lange flexed his brows at Suleka. "What?"

She leaned in and whispered ominously, "She had those gourds of hers in the trunk of her car earlier. I know because I saw them."

Lange pictured back to when they were in the driveway, Suleka talking on the phone by the Taurus. They heard Mary Lynn's footsteps and eased apart. "Here you go," she said, breezing into the kitchen and handing Lange a flowery post-it note with an address on it. "I'll be there from one till about four this afternoon."

"Thanks," said Lange, moving immediately towards the door into the yard. "Have fun at the party," he remarked and threw her one last smile before stepping out into the sunshine.

"Say happy birthday from me," he heard Suleka add and then her footsteps on the gravel behind him. The sun was high in the sky and he felt an overwhelming urge to strip down to t-shirt and shorts and sit out on his log pile, reflecting. He had a lot of information to sift through to solve this case and not much time if he wanted to solve it successfully. "Good catch," he said to Suleka as they buckled up.

"What?"

"The gourds."

She made a pensive grunt, "Hmm," then backed up the Nissan to turn around. "She could have just told us she took them."

"And she could have just told us about going over to Margi's house and seeing that note."

"You know what I think?" said Suleka. She drove to the end of the driveway and stopped. "I think she was embarrassed."

"About what?"

"She took Margi's gourds to the retreat because they were better than hers, and maybe even passed them off as her own because she got the impression from that note that Margi *wouldn't* be back. That's why she didn't tell us."

Lange faced her, interested.

"Think I should call Charlotte, see if she'll ask her guest who Mary Lynn said painted those wolves?"

"Okay. But after we go back to my place."

Suleka was surprised. "We're not going to talk to Sam Breckenridge?"

"Not yet. I want to check my trail camera first."

"You don't think it's too soon?"

Lange smacked his lips together. "I think the man in the mud room was heading in the direction of my yurt when I saw him."

*****

But they didn't get as far as Lange's yurt. Part way up Sauk Mountain Road, Lange caught sight of a longhaired shadow pacing through the woods, heading towards his property. For the second time that morning he leapt out of the Nissan and gave chase. Only once he was under the trees and moving through the brush, he realized he didn't have to move so fast. He could hear the man kicking through the fallen autumn leaves and see his shape threading left and right through the trees but he wasn't moving very fast, almost as though he didn't expect Lange to keep chasing him. He was short, maybe five foot six, squarely built, wearing old jeans and a drab, olive green parka that looked too thin to have any warmth left in it. His dark hair straggled down his back, to just below his shoulders and as Lange followed him through the woods, gaining on him, he could smell marijuana as if it were being expelled through his pores, like sweat.

He came within a dozen steps of the man and called out, "I just want to talk to you." Seconds later the man glanced back over his shoulder, then dodged behind a tree and stopped, as if he were hiding. Lange stopped too. He was panting from pushing hard over the uneven ground and he could hear his breath filling the absence of sound in the forest around him as he observed the frayed tops of the man's sneakers poking out from the base of the tree and the blackened fingers pulling nervously at the cord around the bottom of the parka. His mind raced with his breathing, wondering what he was going to say to this fellow. He didn't want to reprimand him for stealing his milk and he didn't care about the other petty thievery either; but if he'd hurt Margi, well that was something different. He waited for his breathing to calm down, then took one slow step to the left. The profile of the man's face came into view. Lange saw a receding hairline, a pug nose and a salt and pepper beard that curled up at the end. He also saw a beady eye staring off into the distance as the man worried his lips back and forth and up and down.

"You're on my property," Lange said finally, thinking he might lull the man into believing he just wanted to talk trespassing. But he got no reaction. He waited, wondering what to do next, then decided he had no choice; he stepped forward. The man's face spun towards him, filled with fear, and almost as quickly he was off again, hustling easily through the woods. "No, wait!" Lange called out and sprinted after him, left and right, through some second growth cedar trees, then headlong into a small stand of alders. It was obvious this was a trail the fellow had followed before by the surety of his movements and the break in the brush. Lange pushed the pace behind him and was almost within touching distance when they broke out onto the road on his property and found Suleka, leaning against the driver's side door of the Nissan. "Why, Joe!" she declared, at the sight of the bearded man suddenly in front of her. "It's *you!*"

The man swung around to end up on Suleka's left side and edged in tight against her, like a child looking for protection. "It's okay," she said to the right side of his face. She pointed at Lange. "He's not going to hurt you."

Lange looked at her, expectantly. "This is Joe," she explained. She touched the other man on his shoulder. "Joe, this is Cal Lange. But maybe you knew that?"

Joe nodded, a short, curt nod, then sneaked a glance over at Lange. Suleka leaned towards Lange and dropped her voice. "He used to live up the Cascade but his lady friend died a year ago and he hasn't been seen there for a while." She looked at the man standing next to her again and raised her voice. "Did you move away from your place, Joe?"

"Had to," the little man said, his speech nasal, exaggerated. "There were people in the woods behind me, spying."

"Spying?"

"Uh-huh. With those listening devices. You know. Look like snakes?"

Suleka scrunched her face up, skeptical. "You sure?"

Joe nodded vigorously. "I saw them. In my firewood piles."

A quick glance from Suleka to Lange, which he answered with a widening of his eyes. She focused on Joe again. "So where are you living now?"

He waved off to her right. "Over there."

"The Rockport-Cascade Road?" Lange asked. Joe looked at him, then at Suleka.

"The Rockport-Cascade Road?" she repeated. Joe shrugged and nodded at the same time. She glanced at Lange. "He doesn't hear so well so you either have to talk into his right ear, which is his better ear, or make sure he can read your lips." She focused once more on the man standing up against her, and spoke slowly, clearly. "You could've told me you needed milk."

Joe looked anxiously at Lange.

"I don't care about the milk," Lange stated clearly, now that he had Joe's attention. "I just want to know about the woman."

Joe's eyes narrowed, appraising.

"You know the one I mean?"

"Bicycle woman?" Joe ventured.

"Margi," Suleka corrected with an edge of irritation in her tone as if she'd really expected Joe to remember this. "You know, the one lives over by Illabot Creek with Sam."

"I didn't hurt her," Joe countered.

"Is she hurt?" Lange asked.

Joe watched him for a second then shook his head slowly, no.

Lange could tell that he knew something and as long as he didn't push it, he might tell him what he knew. But he had to tread cautiously. "We need help finding her."

"I didn't do it."

Suleka's eyebrows shot up, like she hadn't been expecting this.

But Lange went with the flow. "We don't think you did," he said. "We just need to know where she is." He waited while Joe assessed him warily, then tried again. "Do you know where she is?"

Joe nodded, yes. "I saw where that woman put her."

"Which woman?" pressed Suleka.

Joe frowned, lifting his shoulders up to his ears, and opened his eyes wide, like he didn't know.

"What did she look like?" Lange asked.

Joe's eyes became unfocused, as he contemplated his answer. "Like a scarecrow."

"Shelby," whispered Suleka and Lange could tell she was visualizing the mop of untamed dark hair on the girlfriend's head.

For a moment there was nothing but stillness, like someone had hit pause and locked them all in place. The noontime sun was beating down on their scene and Lange felt way too hot dressed the way he was. He sucked on his retainer and wanted to lower his eyelids and drift away but a chattering of angry birds chasing away a bigger bird above their heads, brought him back to the scene at hand. "Were they on foot or in a car?" he asked.

"Car."

Callum Lange felt a thrum of excitement inside his chest. "What kind of car?"

Joe looked sure of himself for the first time. "Ford Taurus," he declared. "Grandma's……"

"Taxi!" Lange and Suleka joined in.

They beamed at each other as if figuring it out had been a challenge that they'd mastered together and now they were proud of themselves. But then Lange saw Suleka's smile fade and her brows move slowly together as she realized that this meant her friend had done something wrong. Maybe very wrong. Her features changed again, becoming more confused, indicating her mind was questioning what she was thinking. "But why would Mary Lynn…..?" she wondered, to no one in particular.

"Let's not assume anything," Lange told her, stretching a hand out in her direction. "Let's find out." He made sure Joe could see his lips again. "Where did they go in Grandma's Taxi?"

"Power lines road."

"The one that crosses Rockport-Cascade?" Suleka asked.

Joe nodded. "I can show you."

"Please do." Lange didn't waste any time. He strode around the back of the Nissan and threw open the passenger door for Joe but when he looked back, he saw the little man was climbing into the bed of the pick-up. He didn't argue. "May not be legal," he told Suleka as they got in the front at the same time, "but I suspect he's more comfortable back there."

She was still too dazed by the situation to be worrying about where Joe road in the truck. "I thought for sure he was talking about Shelby," she said, backing down Lange's driveway. "Mary Lynn's kind of tidy to be described as a scarecrow."

"Maybe not if she's been wrestling a dead body around."

Suleka shot him a horrified look. "You think Margi's dead?!"

"He said she wasn't hurt."

"That doesn't mean she's dead! Maybe Mary Lynn just drove Margi somewhere to hide, while she figured out what she wanted to do about Sam and Shelby."

"Then why didn't she tell us that?"

Suleka's frustration became evident. "I don't know! I'm not a detective. Why don't you tell me what *you* think?"

"I think I should call Detective Deller, have her get a search warrant for Mary Lynn McCracken's car."

But he didn't need to. Because as soon as they reached Highway 20 again, his phone rang.

It was Deller.

*****

He answered at a clip. "What's going on?"

"I've got news," said Deller, sounding like she was walking through a wind tunnel.

"Us too. You go first."

"The lab got back to me and there's blood on that length of vine maple you picked up from under my car."

"Whose blood?"

"Don't know that yet. We're going to need a sample of Margi's if we're to make that match. But the lab technician did say it's human, because the blood we got from down by the creek was deer blood so she made a point of checking what was on the vine maple."

"Deer blood?"

"Mixed with cat hairs so my guess is it was a cougar kill and the Search and Rescue dogs got distracted by the scent." The wind tunnel died down and Lange heard a jangling, followed by a toc and the squeaky sigh of vinyl being sat on. "What have you got?" Deller asked and he heard her slam a car door creating silence around her voice.

"We caught up with the petty thief and he's taking us to the road that services the power lines off the Rockport-Cascade Road. He says he saw a woman being 'put' there."

"Uh-oh."

"Mmm hmm."

"Was the woman Margi?"

"Sounds like it, yes."

"Any sense of what he means by put?"

"Yes, but…" Lange looked across at Suleka. She was leaning forward over the steering wheel, her hands clutching it tightly, and he got the impression she was lost in her thoughts. But she had an uncanny intuition when it came to tuning into conversations so he swiveled away from her and mumbled into the phone. "I'm going to wait and see before I confirm that sense."

"Who put her there?"

"Mary Lynn McCracken. At least it was her car he saw." Lange looked down as they crossed the Skagit yet again and saw two men, standing on the bank, watching the river go by in front of them. Probably thinking it wasn't a good day to fish, he thought; not with the water so murky.

Deller interrupted his thoughts. "This is the guy that's been stealing food from people's houses in that area? You're sure it wasn't him put Margi on that power lines road?"

"That's not the sense I get."

"So you trust him?"

"Enough to get a search warrant for McCracken's car."

"You're thinking blood in the trunk?"

"Now that I know about the vine maple I am."

Deller sighed, a long, sad expulsion of air. "Okay, I'm on it. And I'll send Deputy Collins to join you on the power lines road. What about Sam Breckenridge? Should Collins bring him along too?"

"Maybe not. It won't be pleasant if Margi's been out there since Saturday."

"Unless she's alive."

"Don't go soft on me now."

He heard the jangling sound again followed by the low growl of an engine. "I'm not soft," she told him. "Just hopeful."

They hung up at the same time and Lange pushed his phone into his jacket pocket. His fingers felt a slip of paper and he remembered McCracken giving him the address of the birthday party in Birdsview. He pulled the phone back out and checked the time; 12:10 pm already. He pulled the paper out of his pocket and began to copy the address into a text to Deller.

"I didn't see any blood in the trunk of Mary Lynn's car, you know," Suleka volunteered from beside him.

His fingers hovered over the tiny keyboard on his phone as he wondered how she knew what Deller had said. "Maybe the tray of gourds was covering it," he replied and went back to typing.

"Margi never hurt anyone that I know of. It doesn't make sense that Mary Lynn would want to kill her."

"Murder often doesn't make sense."

"For psychotics maybe. But why would someone like Mary Lynn…..?"

Lange pushed send, watched the message change color and then slipped the phone back into his pocket. He looked at the skinny trees on his side of Hwy 530 again and thought about how many times Suleka had driven this stretch of road to take care of his needs. Maybe it was time to take care of hers. "Here's what I think happened," he started and watched Suleka's grip on the steering wheel relax as she leaned back in her seat. "I think Margi wasn't depressed at all; she was happy. I think she got that angry letter from Shelby and showed it to Sam and he blew it off. Told her not to worry about it; that the affair was over. Maybe he even told her he was planning to end it when he went away with Shelby that weekend. Who knows? But I think he was planning to give Margi that ring he'd bought because he'd seen something new in her. A spark. She was good at painting those wildlife gourds and she was feeling it. I could feel it when I touched them. And Sam could feel it too. And he was proud of her. I heard it in his voice when he was telling me about her artwork. So he tells her not to worry, that she should go to the retreat while he went and dumped Shelby and that when he got back he wanted to take her out, give her something special. I don't know, that's just conjecture on my part. But it feels right. So Margi calls up Mary Lynn on Friday night and says she wants to go to the retreat and could they ride together? Mary Lynn says of course and maybe they talk about taking their wildlife gourds to sell them, maybe they don't, but either way, when Mary Lynn shows up on Saturday, Margi shows her the box of gourds she plans to take up to the retreat. And the Machiavellian part of Mary Lynn rears its ugly head. She sees dollar signs when she looks at Margi's gourds. She sees art that is way better than anything she could ever make and *she* wants the glory. It's not fair that it go to a mousey little woman who's perennially poor and who can't even keep a husband from straying. So when Margi leans over the trunk of her car, to put something in or rearrange something that's already in there, Mary Lynn sees her chance and smashes her over the head with a thick branch of vine maple, killing her." Lange softened his eyes as he looked at Suleka. "That's all it took."

"How would she know how hard to hit her?"

"She wouldn't. But she couldn't risk Margi coming around to point the finger at her, or get the money she planned to make off her gourds. So she hit her hard enough to make sure there were no repercussions. I imagine Margi fell forward into the trunk, Mary Lynn scooped her legs in behind her, put her wildlife gourds in the car somewhere and then walked through the cabin to see if there was anything else she could take while she was at it. She was thinking artwork, I imagine, but when she found the ring, she couldn't resist."

Suleka's mouth dropped open once again. "You think she took the ring too?"

"I'm not sure. But I'm betting it turns up in the search Deller does of her car. Or her house."

"What about the note?"

Lange shook his head. "There never was a note. Mary Lynn made that up to implicate Sam, something I expect she thought up when she was doing her walk through of the cabin. She also called Margi at that time, evidence that she tried to track her down, and heard the phone ringing in Margi's purse on the counter."

A small knock on the back window of the cab made them both glance over their shoulders. Joe was peering at them, pointing an index finger off to their right. Suleka acknowledged his message with a hand up in the air and then did almost a complete U-turn onto a dirt and gravel lane climbing the ridge they'd been driving alongside. "You know," she told Lange as the Nissan began bumping through potholes, "you're making Mary Lynn sound a lot smarter than I ever thought she was."

"We used to say, when I was on the job in New York, that if criminals put their brains to good use instead of bad, they'd be some of our most successful citizens."

They rode in silence for a good long while, seeing the power lines coming towards them and the road stretching away into the distance above them. The path was dry and grey, a desolate, well-hidden utility road in the midst of land that had been logged and replanted, its short, scraggly trees providing cover on both sides of them. The sun bounced off every ounce of autumn gold on the hillside ahead of them, sending rays of warmth into the solemn quiet of the truck, then the Nissan lugged up around a hairpin turn and Lange saw the sign he had been dreading. Ravens, blue jays and a couple of bald eagles circled in the sky above a steep drop off on the downhill side of the vehicle. "Brace yourself," he said softly to Suleka. But she had seen the carrion feeders too and let the truck roll to a stop even before Joe hammered on the window again. Lange threw open his door and they both heard Joe shout, "That's where the Grandma Lady dumped the body." They looked back to see him pointing over the side.

"Do you have cell service here?" Suleka asked Lange.

He pulled his phone out of his pocket and looked. "Yes. Why?"

"Call Deller and get her to bring Coco, would you?" She looked at Lange, her brown eyes moist with feeling. "Margi would have like that."

He dialed Deller's number as Suleka slowly opened her door.

Made in the USA
Middletown, DE
15 July 2015